ARTICLES OF WAR

For John and Carol,

With all best wishes,

ARTICLES OF WAR A NOVEL **NICK ARVIN**

Yours,

Nick Arvin

3.28.05

DOUBLEDAY

New York   London   Toronto   Sydney   Auckland

PUBLISHED BY DOUBLEDAY
a division of Random House, Inc.

DOUBLEDAY and the portrayal of an anchor with a dolphin are registered
trademarks of Random House, Inc.

This book is a work of fiction. Names, characters, businesses, organizations,
places, events, and incidents either are the product of the author's
imagination or are used fictitiously. Any resemblance to actual persons,
living or dead, events, or locales is entirely coincidental.

Book design by Elizabeth Rendfleisch

Library of Congress Cataloging-in-Publication Data

Arvin, Nick.
Articles of war : a novel / Nick Arvin.
p. cm.
1. World War, 1939–1945—France—Fiction. 2. Americans—France—
Fiction. 3. Women refugees—Fiction. 4. Cowardice—Fiction.
5. Soldiers—Fiction. 6. France—Fiction. I. Title.

PS3601.R77A89 2005
813'.6—dc22
2004050471

ISBN 0-385-51277-5

PRINTED IN THE UNITED STATES OF AMERICA

February 2005

First Edition

1 2 3 4 5 6 7 8 9 10

for
Carl and Dorothy
&
Peter and Carol

There never was a war
that was not inward.

—MARIANNE MOORE

How can I tell you how humbley sorry I am for the sins Ive committed. I didn't realize at the time what I was doing, or what the word desertion meant. What it is like to be condemned to die. I beg of you deeply and sincerely for the sake of my dear wife and mother back home to have mercy on me. To my knowledge I have a good record since my marriage and as a soldier. I'd like to continue to be a good soldier.

Anxiously awaiting your reply, which I earnestly pray is favorable, God bless you in your Work for Victory:

I Remain Yours for Victory

Pvt. Eddie D. Slovik

[LETTER TO GENERAL EISENHOWER, DECEMBER 9, 1944]

ARTICLES OF WAR

1.

THE BOY THEY CALLED HECK ARRIVED AT OMAHA BEACH IN August 1944. Soon he would be sent to the front, but for now he waited for his papers to be processed at the Third Replacement Depot. He felt lonely, nervous, bored. Men were everywhere here, unloading supplies, bringing in artillery and armor, moving off for the front, coming back bandaged or in boxes, or, like Heck, waiting. The scene had a hivelike quality, vehicles and men streaming through this portal into and out of the interior of France. Amid all the activity, with everything in transition, it was easy to feel alone. Men were sent forward every day; every day new men arrived. While he awaited orders Heck had few demands on his time. He wandered the crowded, churned sand of the beach, watched the ships slowly come and go, watched the formations of Allied planes pass overhead, their multitudinous drone burrowing into his bones, their glinting wings and bodies like the crosses of cemeteries. Around him Heck saw men who had lost as much as a hand or an eye who smiled at the prospect of going home. He saw the drivers of the army's ubiquitous two-and-a-half ton trucks poring over their maps with the intensity of generals preparing for battle, and a GI told him that when getting off one of these deuce-and-a-half trucks an infantryman could calculate precisely how much danger he was in by watching how fast the driver turned around and got out of there. The landscape along and just beyond the beach had been reduced to a shambles of destruction—many locals had been living for a couple of months in tents set up inside houses without walls or ceilings while others patched their war-wounded homes with scavenged wood and bits of cloth. They stood sullenly in lines waiting for the soldiers to distribute food to them, and they looked at Heck without pleasure or greeting. It appeared they had had enough of armed combatants of any sort. Sometimes one could purchase from them a kind of hard cider with an under flavor like spoiled milk. Heck could not wait to be sent forward and he dreaded being sent forward: the two emotions alternated and on occasion commingled into a single piercing physical ache. He tried to listen only to his ennui and to have no other feeling.

At his first meal in the mess tent the men had been discussing a replacement who had shot himself in the foot. A large group of GIs were loud and indignant, and they hooted when one of them mocked in a simpering tone the wounded man's woeful tale of a weapon that had discharged while he was cleaning it. The comment of a sergeant, shaking his head over the mess that the replacement had made of his foot, was repeated: "You at least could have taken off your boot and sock first." However, Heck also heard four or five soldiers asking each other, softly: What were the chances that this man would have to go before a court-martial? Would his foot heal up? Would he be treated differently in the hospitals? If he got prison time, how much? Through the discussion ran an implication that whatever the wounded man's fate might be, it would likely be better than ending dead at the bottom of a muddy hole in an anonymous field in northern France. Heck listened and tried to give no sign of listening.

WHEN HE HAD been drafted Heck was already strong from summers of farm labor. He had always been tall. By nature he knew how to accept orders, even exasperating or obviously unnecessary orders, and he knew how to work uncomplainingly at tedious and exhausting tasks. He could shoot a gun. He felt a personal belief in the value of work and discipline. Watching some of the men struggle in training he had experienced a mild contempt. While others complained and swore bitterly, it all seemed to him simple, empty, dull. At the same time, however, he felt uncertain of himself. He knew that the training was just playacting, and the thought of a real battle created a fear in him—a fear he tried to avoid by directing his attention to the details of his tasks.

He felt self-conscious about his voice, which contained a rural Iowa accent. Most of the other GIs seemed far more sophisticated and worldly than himself, even if they hadn't fired a gun before. Heck tended to speak softly. He was balding already, and although he was just eighteen many of the other GIs assumed he was older than themselves. He listened to the conversations around him and watched the card games but rarely participated. But he did what he could to help, pointing out an open button on his neighbor's shirt prior to inspection, helping another who couldn't get the pieces of his M-1 together again after a cleaning. The other men didn't seem to know quite what to make of him, and accepted his help with uncertain smiles. They called him Heck because he never cussed. He knew he seemed an odd character, with his quiet and his air of indifference, but he felt he didn't know how to be otherwise. Sometimes he envied the men who talked and joked together so easily. But there were also times, numerous enough, when he scorned the easy and false companionships he saw among the men around him. Solitude seemed to him to be his natural condition.

When he had completed training he was given a short leave and he went home. He arrived alone at the familiar little house and waited the rest of the day for his father to come home from work. In the window the sky deepened to black. When his father finally came in, they embraced, and Heck felt uncomfortably large and strong. His father seemed pale and exhausted. He asked Heck why he had not turned on the lights, and Heck shrugged.

His father and a partner wrote and published the county newspaper. For as long as he could remember, Heck and his father had woken early every morning and eaten breakfast together. Then his father went to the newspaper office and most often he did not return again until eight or nine in the evening, or later. He kept books and magazines piled in stacks and heaps like small hills around the house. Heck had explored all of them. He was an only child. During the first dozen years of his life they had moved every year or two in search of work, around the Midwest and the Plains States, disrupting Heck's friend-ships each time; he had learned to do without.

His father had a small round potbelly, but otherwise was pale, thin, and rather short, so Heck's size seemed to have come from his mother. She had been a woman of great power in the shoulders and arms, taller than her husband by several inches, with a thick face and wide hips. She was moody. When her mood was good, she would joke and laugh with great energy, and whatever small thing was at hand she would toss over and over again into the air. When her mood was poor she said little, her expression turned dour, and her movements became eco-nomical. Heck always sought to keep her mood up. Even when he had grown as tall as she was, she never ceased to address him as though he were still very small. "Baby" was what she called him, fondly, and in her good moods she would narrate what-ever she was doing as though he were in a swaddled bundle at her breast. "Now we're going to heat some water, Baby. And now while the water is heating we'll clean some space on the counter—" And Heck, sitting at the kitchen table with a maga-zine, felt reassured listening to her.

When he was fourteen, his mother died, very suddenly, of a cancer. It happened in the springtime, and Heck's father soon returned to his work. He hired a woman to clean on weekends, and he sometimes came home even later in the evenings with the smell of whiskey on him, but his established routines were otherwise unaffected. Heck, however, abruptly stopped reading the books and magazines and newspapers around the house that he had pored over in the past. The meanings of the words had suddenly become strangely variable, as if they crawled on the page like ants. That summer he began to find work on the farms outside town. He engaged the labor with steady resolve, and because he worked hard he found himself accepted. He felt he fit in. He often returned home nearly as late as his father did. He was already tall, and now the work created muscles that filled out his form.

After the daily, inflexible routines of army training camp, his week at home felt like nothing but a period of empty waiting. Heck did not tell his father about his new nickname, and everything here seemed to be just as it always had been. His father still had his way of smiling that appeared apologetic, or half sad. Heck went a couple of times to the little cemetery where his mother was buried. To earn extra money he worked for several days on one of the farms. It was summer and they were happy for the help.

He felt glad when the day to depart came. His father took the time off work, and Heck rode beside him in the old Packard toward the train station in Des Moines. Heck's duffel bag could be heard rolling and sliding in the trunk. The farmland around them curved like the fabric of a vast wind-whipped flag. His father said, "This war can't go on forever."

"No. It can't," Heck said. He added, "I'll be all right." His father had been too young for the Great War. When Pearl Harbor had been bombed and America had declared war, Heck had assumed that he would miss this war in the same way. He had not grasped then that a war could go on for years and years.

The windows were open and air tumbled into the Packard, moist and thick with the smell of earth. Waves of heat distorted the line of the road. Heck looked at his father and saw he was crying. He looked away. He had seen his father cry only two or three times before and the image now made him feel both heartbroken and strangely exhilarated. He was uncertain whether he ought to cry too.

After a moment, however, he realized that he did not feel any tears in himself. Instead he felt only a nervous agitation—a vibration in his stomach distinct from and more subtle than the rattling of the Packard. He had no real desire to go to war, but if he must then he wanted to do it quickly. He did not, after all, know what else he wanted to do with his life. Still, it seemed strange he could be sent to war. In truth, he thought of himself as hardly more than a boy, and he possessed an instinctive self-awareness of his own ignorance about many things.

His father said, "Keep your hands clean. Do what they tell you; don't do anything stupid. Remember there's a difference between being brave and being stupid."

"I will." The advice seemed a sign of his father's distress; his father never gave general advice like this. His advice was rare and always specific.

"Look sharp and be sharp."

"I will."

They came into town and drove between long rows of two-story brick buildings and storefronts. They parked at the train station and sat on a bench in the sun and waited. The train was late. They sat fidgeting, the duffel bag between them. Heck's father got up and paced and kicked small stones with the toe of his shoe. His tears were gone.

"Dad," Heck said, "why don't you go on home."

"Ah, no," said his father.

"You don't need to wait here with me, doing nothing."

His father glanced at his watch.

"I know you have work that needs to be done," Heck said.

"Maybe I better," said his father.

Heck stood, they shook hands, and his father got in the Packard and left. Heck was relieved. He waited for the train alone and when it came the car he sat in was empty and this made him happy.

He traveled by train to Chicago, then New Jersey, and a Liberty ship carried him from a Hudson River pier into the Atlantic. He had never seen the ocean before. It was an incredible sight, the sea, which he had read of so often, more vast and mutable than anything he had imagined. When the enormous ship heaved and moved under him he had the sensation of transition, of leaving behind not only a continent but all his past as well. He felt the life he was abandoning now to be a mystery to him, as if he were somehow disassociated from it, and it appeared very small to him and easily left behind. And yet, the open space and the immeasurable sky at sea also reminded him of home. He stood on deck and gazed, recalling intensely the brown-black fields, furrowed and moist with spring rain, things happening invisibly beneath the surface, seeds exploding in slow motion, life struggling toward open air. Open spaces seemed to him particularly ennobled, as if God hovered down closer to such places. Many of the soldiers on the ship were violently seasick, wracked with convulsions and fevers and diarrhea and retching such that they could not even crawl from their bunks to the mess for food, food that anyway would not have remained long in their stomachs. Heck was surprised he did not share their fate, but the motion of the ship did not bother him at all.

What he moved toward, however, remained a great enigma. He understood he might never return to America, that indeed he might die. These were true possibilities. He looked around and said to himself, These men don't truly understand that they might die—they don't truly believe it, in their hearts they believe *It won't be me*—but I understand, it is true, I could die. Understanding this made him especially quiet and still. He began smoking cigarettes. As often as possible he went up to the deck and stood at the rail to watch the sea. On a cloudless day, with horizon in all directions, it appeared they had arrived into the center of eternity. At night it would have been easy to believe that the innumerable stars themselves, not the ship, were swaying. Below him, the wave tips caught the moonlight and winked with the patterns of a complex intelligence. By day the waves carved countless, relentless, boundless sculptural forms, and the water acquired every conceivable shade from black to white and blue to green and, lit by the fires of sunset or the embers of sunrise, violet to scarlet to gold to mud to orange. Heck could gaze upon this extraordinary expanse and achieve a quietude from within which he might contemplate his approaching fate without fear. Indeed, he thought he had defeated his fear entirely, but he was wrong in this, for as soon as he was belowdecks, away from the hypnotic quality of the waters, the fears resurged. I should have been a sailor, he thought, and I never would have been afraid.

As it happened, his first sight of France—the lowering sandy hills over Omaha Beach—was a familiar one. Several times already he had seen the same image in the newsreels.

THE RAINS IN NORMANDY were irregular but persistent. When it wasn't completely overcast, clouds like islands and continents scudded rapidly overhead and in the gaps between them the sunlight played dramatically. Ferocious winds flew in off the Channel and lashed themselves against the trees and the hedgerows. At dusk, when the winds died, insects could be seen swarming into the sky in columns hundreds of feet high. Viscous black mud lay everywhere underfoot, like stuff coming up from a netherworld, and many of the open places had been horrendously cratered and transformed into muddy alien landscapes. The roads were churned and sometimes impassable and the detours only created newly muddy and equally impassable tracks. In the bivouac where Heck had his bunk, the paths between the rows of tents and from the tents to the latrines were stinking mires. Clothing and leather and packs and paper felt sodden; cigarettes grew flaccid; pits of rust appeared on unoiled steel.

Each morning Heck reported for a roll call where some of the waiting replacements were pulled out by number and name, assigned to a unit, given orders, and sent toward the front on a deuce-and-a-half. The mechanisms of the army bureaucracy were beyond logical penetration and these processes had the air of a lottery of ill fortune. Some men were sent forward after only a day or two at Omaha while others had already loitered here for two or three weeks. Occasionally Heck was pulled into some task—KP, perhaps, or unloading rations and ammunition from a truck or landing craft—but until the lottery picked his number he largely existed in a military limbo, essentially without responsibility or practical direction. He passed day to day in tedium and nervous anticipation, in the tent and on the beach where the army's machines and supplies and refuse were spread. At times Heck wanted badly to get away from it. He began to wander down along the coast or into the countryside. This was discouraged, but no one really cared. He had the feeling of walking in a place not quite real, a place strange and boding, as if he had stepped into the geography of some relentless dream. The sandy cliffs rose sharply over the Channel waters, and inland lay wide wheat fields and cow pastures demarcated by tall hedgerows—impenetrably dense tangles of shrubs and trees and vines that grew along the backs of low, long earthen mounds two or three feet high. Many of the hedgerows showed torn and broken gaps where they had been blasted open with explosives or run through by a tank. The elegant spires of the cathedral at Bayeux could be seen from miles around. Roofs were made of slate, and the architecture—even of the barns and the cowsheds—was always of stone, an ash-blond limestone cut with great precision so that the corners of the buildings were defined by sharp right angles. The people seemed small; the older men wore jackets and ties and the younger men wore short sleeves and berets and watched the Americans gloomily. Heck did not know any French, and he listened to these people talking with some awe, some distrust—a part of him had trouble believing people could communicate by sounds so alien. And all around lay the detritus of war, scattered along the beaches and across the fields and into odd corners of the countryside: discarded gas masks, tires, gasoline cans, empty food tins and cartons, fallen telephone cables, parachute containers, deserted gun emplacements, overturned and exploded transports and boats and tanks, rolls of concertina wire, stacks of life belts, mildewed underwear. Homes reduced to door frames. Burned and abandoned bulldozers. The skeletons of goats, cows, dogs, horses. Plastic sheets and bags in all sizes. Paper handbills and flyers strewn amid smashed furniture, fragments of shattered glass. In town the treads of passing tanks were rapidly destroying the cobbled streets. The fallen shop buildings and churches and hotels and houses had the appearance of sand castles bludgeoned by a wrathful child.

One day, after having idled more than a week at Omaha, Heck followed along the coastside cliffs and beaches a couple of miles, then turned inland. He passed through a muddy wood, skirted the high grasses of a swampland, then followed a narrow cart path through several pastures. A skinny goat watched him as he passed. It seemed he had entered a place where the war had not encroached. It was, he thought, very beautiful. He sat for a few minutes on a broad, dry stone and watched a pair of rabbits foraging in a meadow. He smoked a cigarette. He stood again and followed a long hedgerow until it ended among some trees and he worked his way through these until he could see out into another meadow, where a German airplane had fallen. It lay on its belly, and the wings and tail section were gone, the fuselage blackened around the engine and cockpit. Small white clouds scurried by, orchestrating rapid passages of light and shadow, and the wind pushed gently at Heck making his eyes water, so that when he saw a shape moving in the plane's cockpit he thought at first it was an illusion of the wind, the tears, and the shadows of the clouds. But as his eyes cleared the figure failed to dissolve—it was a small, rounded shape, bobbing up and down in the airplane cockpit. The more Heck studied it, the more he thought it had to be a person's head. It kept popping up and down, then disappearing for a while, then reappearing. It reminded Heck of a bird, but it was too large. Then a small shape climbed out and began running forward and back along the fuselage and Heck realized it was a child, a boy. Heck could hear faintly the boy shouting. It struck Heck that, for a child, all this mess of war might seem like the equipment of a complicated and marvelous game. Then another figure appeared at the edge of the meadow to the right, a girl or young woman, who called to the boy. Heck turned and started away. He strode quickly, and he was hoping, without knowing or even wondering exactly why, that the boy and the woman had not observed him when there was the convulsive, sharp noise of a detonation, then screams.

Heck ran back to the edge of the field. The boy lay beside a smoking hole in the earth, screaming and flailing. The woman also was screaming, and she was running toward the boy.

Heck stepped forward, then halted. The boy, he guessed, had set off a land mine. Heck began shouting for the woman to stop, and she slowed for a step or two, looking wildly in his direction, then set off running again. Heck gazed in fear at her and the boy, then at the route before him across the field. He could see only densely growing grasses. When he looked up, the girl, running clumsily in her skirts, was already nearly halfway to the boy. Peering again at the grasses just before him Heck could see no glint of metal, no dark line of wire. Gingerly he pushed a foot forward, set it down, brought the other foot up beside it. The boy's screams already seemed to have become something eternal and luminous, thin and bright in the open air.

Then the woman reached the boy and she tried to haul him up by the armpits. The boy's screams redoubled then fell apart into loud sobs while he floundered and she staggered with him a couple of steps. The boy in his panic seemed to be fighting her, and he slid through her grip. She tried again but could only bring his shoulders to her waist. Then she looked over at Heck. She waved and shouted. Blood from the boy stood out brightly on one of her hands.

Heck glanced behind himself. It would probably take at least half an hour to find his way back to someone who could help. The girl continued to yell at him in French, and he couldn't understand her, but it sounded like she was already shouting at him more in anger than in pleading. For a second he swayed forward and back and forward; then something inside unexpectedly released and he began to run toward them. The tall grasses cracked under his boots, each one feeling exactly like a trip wire, so that every step contained several horrible instants during which he fell toward oblivion. The explosion and pain and void, however, did not come. As he reached the girl she alternately smiled and grimaced and yelled belligerently and loudly at him as though he were still somewhere across the field. She was probably sixteen or seventeen years old, only slightly younger than Heck was himself.

The boy's foot was bloody and looked a mess. Heck took off his shirt for a bandage; finally, he felt like he knew what he was doing. He said, "Quiet now, you're going to be fine, you'll be okay," and the boy probably could not understand any of this but his cries fell to a strangled whimpering. The boy's hands and face were marked with black streaks of soot from the airplane, the knees of his trousers were patched, and his hair appeared combed but greasy, unwashed for a week or two. Heck got him into a sitting position, then, with an arm under the boy's shoulders, lifted him upright. The boy bounced on his good foot and moaned. "Be strong," Heck said. "Be a good boy." He looked around, and the girl pulled on his sleeve.

"There," she said, pointing in the direction she had come across the field.

Heck hesitated, still wary of mines. It would be impossible to find the precise route the girl had taken across the field—the grasses had closed over and made it invisible. The way he had come was unmarked now, too, but he thought he could see the point where he had come out of the woods. He had run directly out, on a straight line, and he believed he could re-create it. Also, the woods were nearer in that direction. "We'll go back that way," he said to the girl. "Then we can circle through the woods." Half-carrying, half-dragging the boy he started ahead. The girl put an arm around the boy from the other side, and the three moved together slowly. The boy moaned; the shirt tied around his foot grew red and moist with blood. Heck watched the grasses ahead carefully, not sure exactly what he was looking for. Suddenly, about halfway to the woods, a new thought came to him. He looked at the girl. "You know English."

She kept her face to the ground and did not immediately answer. Her skirts, brushing the boy's injured foot, were becoming bloodied. She said, with a thick accent, "A little English. Yes."

In the woods the branches hid them from the sunlight and Heck had a feeling of being enclosed and having left the danger behind. When the girl pointed and said, "House," he did not protest but helped move the boy in that direction.

Concentrating on helping the boy along, Heck failed to pay close attention to where they were going. They had not walked for long, it seemed, when he looked up and just ahead lay a stone building. It stood in a small clearing among the trees where the weeds and brush had grown so high that the walls of the house were largely obscured. The roof was sagging and had fallen through in a couple of places. As they came up to the door he saw that the windows were gone; some had been boarded up with panels of stained and varnished wood evidently removed from pieces of furniture. They stepped inside, and the walls glistened with water. Spread across the floor were things in sacks and rough bundles, ready, it appeared, to be moved at a moment's notice. Daylight came through the holes in the ceiling, and under the largest of these was an improvised, blackened fire pit. A man rose from a chair in the corner and hurried to the boy. Only when the man had taken the boy and Heck stood watching the two of them, feeling suddenly useless, did he notice that the man had only one arm. The man laid the boy out on a thin paillasse, then ran around the room fetching water and soap and a vial of iodine, tearing a sheet into bandages, all the while shouting at the children in French. He was extraordinarily dexterous with his single hand, able, using his teeth and underarms as anchors, to tie knots and wrap bandages. Heck stood in his dirty undershirt watching while they worked on the boy's foot. When it had been cleaned it actually did not look so bad. The boy's eyes caught the light and shone like beacons while he watched the others work on him.

When he finished dressing the boy's foot, the man stood and, for the first time, looked at Heck. His cheeks were scarred by purplish, pocked tissue that was only poorly obscured by a thin beard. He wore a suit of battered, dark blue wool and a yellowing shirt, open at the collar. His left sleeve was pinned up to the shoulder. He said, unprompted, "Lost it during the previous war with the Germans." He gestured at the pinned sleeve. "You can stare if you like. Nation of brutish engineers, the Germans." He spoke with an odd, pinched, vaguely British accent. "Running forward and back, up to this trench, back to that one. Then an explosion, and I find I've lost the arm. Could've been worse, of course." He laughed, as though this were a joke. "You are American. My name is Albert. What's your name?"

"You're the father? Of the boy, and her?"

"Yes, of course. Please have a seat. She is Claire. The boy is Ives."

Instinctively Heck felt wary of giving his real name. He said, "They've been calling me Heck." He looked at Albert expecting questions, but Albert only nodded.

"Welcome," said Albert, "to our château." Again he laughed.

Heck sat at the small wooden table where Albert had been sitting when they entered. Albert rummaged into a trunk and offered Heck a shirt. It smelled sour and in the stomach was a cigarette burn, but it fit reasonably well. The left arm had to be unpinned. Albert then rinsed Heck's own shirt perfunctorily, and hung it to dry from a coat rack. The bloodstains still showed. Peering through doorways, Heck could see that the rooms farther back lay in ruined, haphazard arrangements of timber, stone, glass, and roof slates. The building had once been fairly large but it seemed only two front rooms survived more or less intact. The girl, Claire, was sitting in a wooden chair, near her brother. Heck watched her a moment then looked down at the table before him. He hoped this was not too obvious. She quietly studied her father or Ives and it was difficult to guess what she was thinking. Then, when Heck looked up, he saw all three of them gazing at him—hungrily, he thought.

"Their mother is dead, of course," Albert said. "I do the best I can. Difficult times." The flesh of his face and his neck drooped a little, as if he had been partially deflated.

"Maybe," Heck said, "the boy should be taken to a doctor for stitches?"

"Quite unnecessary," Albert said. "Not at all. I know there was some blood, which is always rather alarming, but the cuts are shallow. I have dealt with many such wounds." Albert began pacing the room and an element of herky-jerky uncontrol dominated his movements. Heck was not sure if this could be caused by the imbalance of the missing arm. It seemed possible that Albert was somewhat mad. He wheeled round suddenly. "Don't talk very much, do you?"

"Sorry, sir. I'm still catching my breath."

"She's a quiet one too." He indicated Claire. "Ives sometimes talks as if it were necessary as breathing. But not now. Must have put a scare into him. I told you not to be playing in a place like that, didn't I?" He glared at the boy and the boy looked back with a defiant expression. Albert turned again to Heck. "I know what you're thinking. I should keep better watch over my children."

Heck shook his head.

"You are thinking—I would be thinking if I were you—what sort of a father lets his son go out and step on explosives?" He said to the boy, "You're unbelievably lucky the damage was not worse."

The boy appeared unconcerned with any of this. Of course, the father was speaking in English.

"I should be going," Heck said suddenly. "I'll be missed soon." He wouldn't, but he felt uncomfortable here; these people seemed ensconced in some peculiar, haunted world of their own.

"Well," said Albert. He clenched his single hand into a fist, making a large and dangerous-looking object. "Come back to-morrow. We will be prepared for a guest. We will thank you in proper fashion."

"I may not be able to."

19

"My boy, just come. Tomorrow. Please."

Without answering, Heck took his shirt and went to the door. He looked around the dank dwelling one more time. "Perhaps I can get some things for you. I could bring food, clothes. No one's really paying much attention. There's so much stuff passing through."

"No, no," said Albert. "Thank you. We don't need anything."

"Fresh bandages, maybe."

"No," said Albert, waving toward the door. "You've done enough already."

Heck glanced once more at the girl—she was watching him quietly—then turned and stepped quickly out the door. He picked his way through the overgrown, weed-infested lawn of the "château," entered the woods, and stood a moment in indecision. He listened for the ocean or the noise of a road, but could hear only the birds and the wind. Finally he simply picked a direction he hoped would take him back to Omaha and set out, gripping his still wet and bloody shirt in one hand.

When he heard footsteps coming up rapidly behind him, he stopped. After a moment he saw Claire. She affected to be studying things other than him—the leaves, the path. "Hello," he said.

She said, quietly, in her accent, "Hello." Her features were now more calmly composed than they had been when she was helping Ives, and she looked somewhat older, perhaps as old as Heck himself. He wondered how old he appeared to her, and he felt self-conscious of his thinning hair. He was curious why she had followed him, but unsure whether she would understand the question, and how she would take it if she did understand, so they walked on together a while in silence. They were on a narrow, vaguely defined path that evidently had not been much trafficked in a number of years. The girl said nothing. Heck fidgeted with the buttons and cuffs of Albert's shirt. "So," he said, "where are we going?" But Claire glanced around with a look of not understanding. She looked thin—not terribly so, but the angles of her bones showed a little more in her face than they probably would have if she were eating well every day. She had full lips, narrowly set eyes, and a narrow, sharp nose. The flesh immediately under her eyes was the color of faded bruises. She wore her hair short in thick dark curls. On her pale skin, at the line of her chin, were a series of small dark moles and she looked to him not at all like any of the girls he had known back home. She was soon moving through the woods with a quick confidence, and Heck fell slightly behind her. Sunlight sparkled between the leaves overhead. The path took an increasingly erratic course, meandering around trees and slopes so that soon Heck had no idea where it would ultimately lead.

They came to a small glade where the trees ringing around blocked all the sky except for a single porthole at the center. Across the ground grew a thin carpet of grass and mosses. There was a buzzing sound that came, Heck saw, from a series of beehives in a row along one side of the clearing, small wooden structures painted white but peeling and weathering to gray and black.

Claire went to the hives. She seemed to have no fear of the bees, and she opened a door with her bare hands. As she reached inside, the collective whine of the bees altered in pitch and volume, and they began swarming out. In the slant light cast through the opening overhead the stirring, rising bees looked like the sparks of a campfire someone had kicked or prodded. Claire paid them no attention. She closed and latched the hive, and she returned across the glade with a piece of honeycomb in her hand. Or not a honeycomb, Heck saw. It was some other small object, a toy or a box, perhaps—she held it away from him and twisted it in her hands. "What is it?" he said.

She giggled and continued to twist or turn the thing; then with a flourishing gesture she presented it on the palm of her hand, a small ornate silver box playing tiny notes of music. He did not recognize the tune.

She smiled broadly at Heck, offering it to him. He gazed, dumbfounded. She said, "It is named? What? Is called?"

"A music box?"

"A—music—box," she echoed. A fat bead of honey hung from a corner. She wiped it with a thumb and forefinger. Then she took Heck's hand and deposited the music box there.

"No," he said, trying to push it back toward her.

"I give you," she said, licking her fingers.

When he tried again to give it back she stepped away, raising her hands in the air. He looked at the music box. The silver was patterned with entangled scrollworks and arabesques. A tiny latch allowed him to open it and peer at the mechanism inside. It was not much larger than a cigarette lighter. The music slowed then stopped and she showed him where to wind it again and left it playing in his hand, this silver, musical thing, and a happy bewildered feeling rose inside him. "Good-bye," she said, and she waved and walked away, back up the path.

When the music box had slowed and stopped he listened to the quiet and realized he could hear, very faintly, the purr of waves striking the shore.

In the mess tent that evening the army fed Heck with Spam, marmalade, crackers, and thin coffee. It was the same every day. While Heck sat over his dinner at a long wooden table, the man across from him was showing the men to either side a photo of his wife. He seemed to think his wife was something pretty special, and he had a whole monologue going about how beautiful and smart she was. When one of the men set the photo down on the table so he could eat, Heck looked at it and thought she did not look like all that much. He thought of Claire, and Claire won the comparison with the girl in the photo. That evening he lay on his back listening to the creak of the tent canvas as it rocked in the breeze and to the muted indecipherable voices of men whispering around him. He held the music box in his hand, not playing it but feeling the honeyed, tacky surface of it. He recalled the few words Claire had said—*It is named? I give you*—weighed them and examined them like unusual coins. He began to wonder at his behavior in the field, at the airplane. He felt he had done well once he had gotten to the boy. But he also had a desolate and dry feeling as he considered his hesitation at the edge of the field. He wished Claire had not seen him hesitate. He felt woefully young.

The next morning he woke to the sounds of the games of poker and spades that had already begun. Tanks and armored personnel carriers were moving by with noises of grinding and straining metal. Shortly after dawn a vast number of airplanes passed overhead. Eventually the mutters of the card games widened into the shouting, cursing, angry voices of men trying to get things through the physical and bureaucratic morass of the beach. Heck obtained a new shirt from a wooden-faced supply sergeant. It began to rain, and he waited in his tent listening to the drumming of it. Idly, he tried to remember the songs his mother would sing in the kitchen, but he could recall only a phrase or two. He'd never been able to carry a melody himself. In the mess tent at lunch he sat alone. Then he pulled on a plastic rain poncho and set off to find Albert, Ives, and Claire at the château. While he walked the rain slackened to a misting drizzle, then tapered to nothing. Low wraiths of fog rose from the hollows of the land, looking solid and sulky and unlikely to retreat before the feeble sunlight that filtered through the ashen clouds.

They had cooked rabbits—or hares, Heck wasn't sure—two of them, and there was half a wheel of cheese and some cauliflower and a sodden mass of cooked greens of a type that Heck could not identify but he suspected would normally have been classed as a weed. From tin cans they drank cider, which tasted punky. The boy was served on his paillasse and ate voraciously. Albert and the girl and Heck sat together around the small table. Albert's elbow jostled against Heck's. He kept both knife and fork in his hand, switching them deftly between his fingers. "You see," said Albert, "we know how to treat guests when we know to expect them."

He seemed more calm today, less sudden and vehement in his movements. Perhaps the emotion of his son's injury had unsettled him the day before. Still, he was clearly an eccentric. A *character,* Heck thought—his father would have used that word, the implied disapproval curtailed by the belief that the judging of others was a needless and unhelpful habit.

The smoke of the fire did not clear the room easily but accumulated in visible stratifications. Occasionally, Albert got up and stood wagging his hand overhead to direct the smoke toward the hole in the roof. He looked particularly ungainly and extraordinary in this posture. "The Great War," Albert said, sitting again. "I do not understand why they call it that. And what is this then, this thing we have now? What do they call it? Is this the Not-as-Great War, or is it the Even-Greater War?" He gestured slashingly at the stump of his missing arm. "For me it was not such a Great War." He laughed. He spoke in a rambling, desultory way. He said he and the children had been wandering the countryside ever since the June invasion, when their home was destroyed by a stray shell. "It was not such a château as we have here, but the roof was intact, and the walls did not sweat like this." But he also gave the impression of moving from place to place for some time now, years perhaps. Heck wondered if it was the children's mother's death that had unhinged Albert. Or had it been the trenches, the Great War, the loss of an arm?

Without prompting Albert would recommence his meandering talk. "I'm glad to see you because I am glad to be able to speak in English again. When I was a child I had a grandmother who lived with us and would speak nothing but English. She came from Nottingham. She said Shakespeare's language was the only civilized language on earth. In fact she was quite senile and had forgotten her French, which was her second language. I would find her sitting like a child on the floor, scratching naughty English words on the wall with bits of charcoal. From her I learned *fuck, shit, damned bloody hell.* She was stupid as a horse but she lived a long time and spoke nothing but English."

Claire leaned over to her father and whispered. He nodded. "She says you have very good teeth. Like a horse."

Heck smiled, self-consciously, showing his teeth. "Thank you," he said. He looked at Claire. "Thank you." She smiled. Heck reexamined her other features. As she drank the cider, her cheeks grew redder. For a moment Heck tried to imagine how she might look in the pink-and-white frilled dresses the girls back home wore to dances. The juxtaposition was strange and caused him to look down in embarrassment.

"Of course," Albert said, "the Germans took all the horses. She likes horses but thinks only Germans can have them." He stuffed his mouth full of cauliflower and greens. Suddenly, through the greens, he said, "I was an artist, before the Germans came. They didn't know what to make of my paintings, so they burned them, to be safe. You can paint, you see, with one hand. Only need one hand. It's like masturbation that way."

He didn't laugh at this, so Heck didn't smile. "Do you have any left? Paintings?"

"No. I was not great. At painting I mean. At masturbating I am terrific. At painting I would never be a genius, but I was sometimes quite good. People paid money for my paintings from time to time. That's not bad. And the best ones I had kept. The best I did not want to sell. Not yet. I would put together a show of the best, when there were enough of them, and perhaps I would gain some small fame. But the Germans did not understand them. Of course, the paintings did not have anything to do with the Germans. What do I care about Germans? But they looked at me, an artist with my arm obligingly removed by some German lad, and they made their assumptions, and they burned all my work in a big heap in the garden, on the rows of radishes and spinaches we had then. Years of life. Up in smoke. Isn't that a common phrase? Up in smoke."

"I'm sorry," Heck said.

"No," Albert added abruptly. "I don't blame her for leaving." He looked defiantly at Heck.

"Your wife?"

"Yes."

After a minute Albert began talking again. "There's no one to trust. War makes thieves and liars of everyone. Dishonor is everywhere. People will do anything—loot a neighbor's home, murder a grandmother—anything they can think of to help them live a day or two longer. And people are stupid. I'm stupid, you're stupid. These children, bless them, are quite stupid. The best thing to be done is keep to yourself, stay away from all the others, keep the stupidity to a minimum. Because the stupidity accumulates. One or two people are manageably stupid. A handful of people are, collectively, dumb as your average dog. A mob: stupid as an insect. Armies, nations: stupidest things on this earth."

When they had all finished eating, Ives spoke up from his seat in the corner. He glanced now and again at Heck and he talked for a long time, looking sullen, mumbling so that Heck was not sure he could have caught the meaning even if he had understood French. When he had finished, there was a silence. Finally, Heck asked, "What did he say?"

"Thank you," Albert said. "He says thank you." He frowned at the boy.

"For yesterday?"

"Yes."

"Well, you're welcome," Heck said, embarrassed.

He left a few minutes later, after saying good-bye and shaking Albert's hand. "Come back anytime," Albert said with a strange, leering smile. Heck walked through the high weeds and into the trees, then stood, hesitating. Several minutes passed. Finally, he heard someone coming through the weeds, then brushing through the branches of the trees. She stopped before him and spoke, watching his eyes. She was speaking in French, and seemed to be asking a question, a gentle one, and he nodded. She took his hand—her callused flesh harder and bonier than he had expected—and led him through the trees to a rough path through the woods.

They crossed a couple of empty, windy pastures. They skirted a house and a large garden full of round green cabbages. Soon he heard the blood-rushing sound of the ocean. They entered a span of open land before the seaside. Perhaps this land had once been farmed; now however it was overgrown with grasses and a few wind-bent saplings no more than waist-high. Heck began to feel nervous, thinking the Germans would of course have mined these areas along the shoreline, but the girl had his hand and moved confidently. They passed a concrete bunker gazing with its cyclopean eye-slit toward the Channel. Heck was sweating. He wiped at his face with his free hand and saw it trembling slightly.

They sat on a ledge over the sea. All beyond lay water, its gray surface curling and fluttering, sketched with white doodles and dashes of spume. Directly below them the sea boomed and rebounded off black rocks. A fine, invisible mist hovered in the air and blew a chill over the flesh. Claire's skirts fluttered. "America," she said to him.

"Yes, I'm an American."

"Where?" she said.

"America, yes, that's it."

"No. No," she said. "Where America? Where?"

He began to point toward the west, toward America, but she shook her head. "No." She opened her arm out wide. "America." She brought her hands together and gestured in a small circle and looked quizzically at him. "Where?"

"Oh," he said. "Iowa."

"Ohiowa?"

"Iowa. Just Iowa. Iowa."

She said, stretching the syllables, "I-oh-wa."

"Yes." He smiled with a sudden piercing inside, a physical sensation of great longing.

"Beautiful?" she said.

"Yes." He longed for home. He thought of the wide fields he had worked and in their absence seemed to know them with an intimacy he had never felt before.

The gray water merged seamlessly with the gray sky. It would probably rain again soon. Heck thought of winter at home, of the swells and swales of the snowscape under skies clouded horizon to horizon, devoid of form or sun. But here, in the monochrome field of sky and sea, were the narrow, dark gray silhouettes of ships—so many ships that when he scanned them, from one horizon to the other, they were hard to believe. He could not imagine any earthly power that would bear up for long before the colossal quantities of war machinery carried by such a fleet. For a moment he felt good looking at all the ships.

The girl rose and gestured for him to follow. She went along the bluff, then maneuvered onto a narrow ledge that slanted down toward the sea. She followed it with quick, precise steps.

He went after her, moving gingerly, edging his feet along the irregular shelf, seeking foothold to foothold. She had made it appear simple, and as he tried to follow he was astonished by the speed with which she moved.

Then, when he looked over again, she was gone. He called. He twisted to peer downward, toward the water, and saw no sign of her. He looked back the way he had come, then up—and suddenly felt a profound vertiginous fear. The bleak sky was somehow more foreboding than the rustling water below. His voice cracked as he called again.

Now she answered, her voice high and strangely resonant. He still could not see her. He called and she replied again. Suddenly her face appeared out of the rock ahead. She smiled.

He shuffled and clambered over to her. She was on her stomach in the entrance to a cave. The opening was a sort of crooked slit with a jutting lower lip, just large enough that he might be able climb in beside her. He peered into the dark of the cave and hesitated. He could imagine an animal, or a German, biding time in there. The girl said something coaxing in French. With the acid feeling of stepping into a trap, he climbed in.

His ribs and his shoulder touched hers as he lay there, and her flesh moved against his as she breathed. "Pretty," she said, gesturing at the horizon. She glanced at him and he looked away, embarrassed. He stuck his head out beyond the lip of the cave and peered straight down at the water.

When he looked at Claire again she was smiling at him. He

marveled at her smile. He wondered what she was thinking of to bring her this expression. She nudged him and pointed over the water. "Home," she said. "Ohiowa."

He laughed. "Yes," he said. He shaded his eyes and squinted as though he could nearly see it. He waved. "Hello, home."

She waved with him. "Hello, Iowa."

He crossed his arms and set his chin on them and watched the sea. He tried to forget about the war he was to participate in. But it was not easily forgotten—there were all the ships spread before him.

Claire pushed herself up and with a writhing, twisting movement slid over his back and turned herself around. "Come," she called, crawling into the dark. He watched her disappear, then wormed himself around and followed.

He scraped ahead on hands and knees for a few feet; then the space widened and he stopped. After several seconds his eyes adjusted and he could see a little: the cave opened into a small room, not high enough to stand in but enough to sit. Claire's pale face floated amid craggy shadows of varying darkness. Heck felt along the wall toward her, knocking loose gravel as he moved. Claire giggled. Every noise resonated strangely, like an underwater echo. He sat beside Claire, his thigh against hers.

She began to sing, just softly. Perhaps it was a lullaby. He could not interpret the words but the melody seemed dimly familiar. Her voice, whispery and soft, was beautiful. When she finished, he wished he could sing, but all he could remember were the obscene cadences from training camp.

She pushed herself away from him again, and dimly he saw

her cross to the other side of the room. She leaned down and appeared to slither—he saw the shadow of her foot wag amid the shadows—and in an instant she was gone. "Hey," he said.

Her voice came back flattened and distant seeming: "Iowa."

He crab-walked to where she had vanished but could see only the broken, irregular wall of the cave. Then he made out an area to the side where the ceiling and floor narrowed toward each other. It might have been an opening, but he could hardly imagine a human would fit through. He crawled nearer. "Hey," he said.

"Hey!"

He crouched forward, hands on the ground, gazing into the darkness. He heard his own breathing, quick and a little ragged, and felt his heart throbbing. The air seemed thin. He had no particular fear of small places, or darkness, but this—where was she leading him? How deeply into the earth? Someone could put a knife into him in a place like this and no one would ever know or much care. The army would assume he had deserted. Albert would think what a nice American he had been, to give Claire everything in his pockets. Or perhaps Albert had plotted this.

Heck shook his head in the dark, which induced a dizziness.

He felt forward into the crevice. Lying flat he worked ahead with his elbows and knees, feeling blindly with his hands, until he was able to slide under the upper edge of the opening. He heard Claire say: "Iowa?"

"A moment," he whispered.

"A—moment," she echoed.

He pushed himself forward until the entire length of his

body seemed encased in rock. The pressing stone made him breathe raspingly. He began to lunge and flail forward. Suddenly the route ahead was blocked by a wall of rock and he squealed in panic—he was uncertain how he could back out of this position. Already he could imagine starving and dying here. But after twisting and probing for some time he found open space to one side above his head. He wormed over a sort of hump, and emerged blindly into a larger opening.

He probed about with his hands and every surface—the entire discernable universe—was of cold stone. Then his fingers were on soft, warm cloth—Claire's stomach he realized, and he flinched away in surprise. She laughed. In recoiling he struck his head on the ceiling above and cried out. A host of white shapes swirled in the dark.

Claire asked something in French. He said, "I'm okay," feeling his head cautiously, anticipating a lump.

"Okay," she said.

Feeling about with his hands, he found the room to be low and generally circular—pancake-shaped—and perhaps two body lengths across. The floor was relatively smooth. The air was still and cool. He had thought the darkness absolute, but after a couple of minutes he could see a trace of light leaking in the way he had come. It was such a dim smudge that he had to stare at it for some time in order to convince himself that it was not an illusion.

He lay listening. After that first touch on the girl's stomach he had shied away, and now he was not certain of her position. Faintly he heard her breathing and, more loudly, he heard his own breath. Somewhere, occasionally, a drop of water fell. Unless he was gazing directly at the smudge of light where he had come in, it made no difference whether he had his eyes open or closed.

"Iowa," said Claire.

"Yes?" he said.

Her skirts, her blouse and boots rustled and slid. He felt her fingers in his hair and she giggled. She found his arm and lay alongside him with her shoulder, arm, and leg against his. Her stomach made a noise and they laughed. He turned his face toward her, though he could not see her, and said, "Hungry again?" She said nothing, and after a second he realized sadly that she did not understand. But then she pressed nearer to him and suddenly, within the darkness, her lips were on his.

He flinched slightly but her lips quickly found his again. In the eerie cold of the narrow cavern her touch felt rough and hot on his skin. Though they hardly moved, each noise they made against the stone or each other resounded loudly. She shifted and took his ear in her mouth, and he groaned.

Then her stomach grumbled once more and they laughed. Their mouths came together again. He had the odd thought that she might eat him if she could, but then it was forgotten. The cold had gone, and the dark was full of the sensations flowing across his flesh. She smelled of raw soil and cider and like the humid air from off the sea, she smelled sweaty and sweet and human and awful and glorious. She seemed slight in his hands, and he could feel her muscles tense and relax under his fingers. His penis was swollen to the point of aching. He had once lain with Becky Shirley in the bed of a Chevy truck, and they had kissed for what seemed like a very long time. Then Becky sat up and straightened her hair, he drove her home, and after that they could only look at each other with embarrassment. It was his only experience with a girl's body. It was one of the reasons he had little to say to other men: he imagined anything he might say would reveal an embarrassing ignorance.

Becky Shirley's breasts had been large and heavy as fruits. This girl's breasts were small and through her blouse he easily held each under his hand like a palmful of grain. At the center of each he felt the soft-hard pebble of her nipple. She moved her hands under his shirt and slid her fingers lightly over his chest. She began to whisper something in French. It sounded lovely.

He found his way under her blouse with his hands to her naked stomach and back and chest. He could feel the muscles over her shoulders and the knuckles of her spine. The lines of her ribs were each distinct and he traced them with sorrow and desire. She gasped when his hands arrived on the skin of her breasts, the sudden sound of inhalation loud in the dark. He ran his fingers down into the pelt of her pubic hair, and it was as if he had reached down and brushed his fingers upon the root of the world. He froze in that attitude a moment. Her fingers drew together slowly on his back.

He retreated slightly and brought his hand up to touch her face. Blindly he felt the soft outline of her lips, the form of a cheekbone. She whispered something. Drawing a fingertip near her eye, he discovered moisture. He hesitated, then touched near her other eye. Here too he found a small, shallow pool, her tears warm, her eyes closed. She was crying. "Oh," he said. Something small inside his rib cage seemed to turn over, a sensation that then grew, as if unfurling. He recoiled from Claire, and the feeling inside him began pressing outward, but, still, it took him a moment to recognize the sensation as simple fear.

He rolled away and shoved his shirttails into his pants. She uttered a small, despairing sob. "I'm sorry," he said and squirmed around on the stone floor and fled, clumsily, back into the narrow space he had slithered through moments before. Behind him she called, "Iowa? Iowa?" By the time he found his way to the entrance again she sounded as if she were crying and very far away.

He emerged into a rain. It fell thinly and darkened the rock surfaces. When he stretched along the rough ledge they had followed down, he slipped and hung a moment with a foot and hand in space. The surf pounded white below. He brought his body back against the cliff side and forced himself to slow. But soon he was scrambling again. His hands and feet seemed always on the verge of slipping, but he reached the top, pulled himself up by two muddy fistfuls of grass, and ran. When he entered, breathless, the shelter of a few trees the sudden panic that had driven him began to relax, and he slowed to a trot. It was a sublime relief to be free of the lightless cave and have the sky above him again. He stopped and massaged the flesh of his face and discovered himself smiling.

But by the time he had arrived back among the other replacements encamped and waiting at Omaha, any sense of joy had faded. Thinking back, he swelled again with lust and he did not understand anymore his fear. He felt he at least should have waited to be sure the girl made it safely across the rain-slick rock. He should have gone back to check on her.

Trying to distract himself, he got out a piece of paper and tried to think of a letter to write to his father, but his thoughts spun in a manner that made the task impossible, and finally he put the blank page away. He smoked several cigarettes. It began to seem to him that he might be without bravery in any category. He went outside and sat on a crate and watched some of the others playing spades. He gazed at the game but hardly saw or heard a thing, until they began to discuss women. Then he got up and moved away.

The rain picked up again. For a long time he stood above the beach, wearing a plastic poncho, watching the activity and wondering at himself. He took the music box from his pocket and wound it and let it play and slow and stop, then returned it to his pocket. He resolved he would go back to the château the next day and in some way apologize to the girl.

The next morning, however, he and several other men were pulled from the roll call lineup and assigned to the 28th Division. A corporal led them to a pair of waiting trucks, and as Heck sat on the hard benches with the other silent and stinking men he tried to think about where he was going. But the future was obscured by an enormous darkness, and his meager imagination felt like a pathetically small stick to poke into it. He sensed before himself a distinct fate, though he could not see it. He longed to see it. He thought any fate would be easier to accept if only he could know it.

2.

NO ONE IN THE TRUCK SEEMED TO KNOW ANYONE ELSE. THEY
rode in silence for a mile or so; then one man asked for a light,
another wondered aloud if anyone had heard any recent base-
ball scores, and soon several conversations had sprung up.

Heck watched the surroundings. He had taken a position
near the tailgate, where he could, he figured, escape most
quickly if the need arose. He also had a vague notion that he
might be a sort of a hero if he sighted some unexpected danger.
But mostly he was afraid and his fear made his thoughts jumpy.
He seemed possessed of an excess of energy and first one leg
then the other trembled uncontrollably, causing his heel to tap
rapidly on the steel floor. Amid all the truck's jolting, none of
the others appeared to notice.

They passed between hedgerows, then long wheat fields often densely pocked with craters and foxholes and the blackened, twisted, unnatural corpses of tanks and light artillery,

half-tracks and jeeps. In one hedgerow, an American Sherman tank hung precariously in a gap it had created only to meet there its demise. Looking at the disabled German panzer tanks lying about, Heck thought unhappily that they appeared considerably larger and more fearsome than the American Shermans. In training he had been assured that the American tanks were faster and more agile, but when it came down to it, he thought, wouldn't anyone rather have more steel and a bigger gun?

Trees had been blasted and splintered and denuded, barns burned to the ground. Grossly blackened cattle lay swelling. They moved through a village visited by the war, and the devastation made the GIs in the truck silent. Heck had seen destroyed towns in newsreels and in the papers, but he had not understood the scale until now. The destruction was vast, the things and homes of many lives reduced to a great acreage of rubble, none of it reaching higher than eye level. And soon the same firepower that had done this would be aimed at himself. The native French were moving the rubble by hand, sifting through the remains of their homes. They turned long, blank stares on the passing Americans. As the truck exited the far side of the village, a group of boys hurled small, rock-hard apples at them. The fruit made sharp pinging noises off the side of the truck and one soldier was struck on the neck and yelped loudly. No one laughed and no one made any gesture or threat toward the boys, although the GI who had been hit muttered curses implicating the boys' mothers. One towheaded boy seemed to stare directly at Heck and to aim for him particularly, but his apples fell short, and soon the boys had receded from sight.

The road had been torn up by the treads of tanks and the

convoys of supply trucks feeding the front, as well as by the shell craters, which the engineers had hastily filled. The driver of Heck's truck seemed to make wholly arbitrary decisions about which holes to plow through and which to avoid by violent swerving. Heck shifted continually in his seat, but it did little good—already, in every position his flesh felt bruised and raw. He closed his eyes awhile, but the battering caused vivid, malevolent geometries to spiral and throb on the black of his eyelids, and soon he could watch these no longer. He felt ill, and he thought it would be absurd to go across the entire Atlantic without getting sick, only to be hit with it here on a road in France. He tried to follow the advice he had overheard a sailor offer as they crossed the Atlantic: watch the horizon or the sky. The depth of the sky, however, did nothing to console him, and on the horizon bloomed dark clouds of smoke. His eyes had the sensation of being loose in their sockets, as though they would fall out if he tilted his head forward. Inside his gut burned a small hot flame. He held his M-1 between his legs and his fingers on it were moist. Repeatedly he wiped them on his pants.

Then, despite all the distractions, his thoughts turned back to Claire. The night before he had thought of nothing but her. Now, without warning, he felt again her ribs under his hands, heard her breath in his ear. In his pocket was the music box.

He felt like a coward for leaving and abandoning her, but he saw no other choices. I'll have to return and look for her when I can, he told himself. Although, in truth, the idea of seeing her again filled him with profound embarrassment. She would be justified in scorning him after the way he had fled her. But then he seemed to touch again the smooth knuckles of her spine. The presence of her music box in his pocket was comforting. It gave him a secret distinction, separating him from these others, all in the same uniform.

The man across from him began saying, intermittently, "Fuck. Fuck fuck fuck." He gazed down at the barrel of the gun between his legs as a man might gaze at a hole from which he expected a snake to erupt. The man's evident fear irritated Heck, even though he also felt it, and it caused him for some miles to be able to look around with a spirit of contempt. A soldier stood and shuffled unsteadily down the length of the pitching truck, and when he reached the tailgate he urinated onto the passing road. Then he shuffled back to his seat, stepping high over duffel bags and packs, putting his hands on the heads of the seated men. He looked drunk, which Heck attributed to the movement of the truck, but later he noticed this same man tipping a small flask to his lips.

Heck decided that his own fear definitely annoyed him. It felt now like an object, exactly as if someone had cut him open, stuffed this thing inside, and sewn the flesh closed again.

The Germans were using horses to haul their equipment, and soon the animals lay dead and unburied along the road in numbers shocking to Heck. He had been bracing himself for months for the sight of dead men but was unprepared for dead horses. He experienced his first real sentiment of animosity toward the Germans—a horse had even less volition than a soldier, and to send so many of the beautiful animals to a futile destruction was abhorrent. Their bodies were mauled, disemboweled, torn into pieces, they were rotting and swelling hideously. In one place the horses had been piled and were burning, creating streamers of black smoke and a rancid, choking stench worse than any smell Heck had known. As they passed by, one of the bloating horses in the fire exploded with a loud, moist noise.

But the war leaped over the landscape with random and spasmodic wrath, touching earth in one place or another just long enough to crush everything, then vaulting far ahead, and they passed through wide swaths of countryside where no evidence of destruction was to be seen, and there were entire towns where people moved about their daily business quite as if they had never heard of the war. For a time it seemed to Heck that his senses had drifted somewhat away from the sickening discomfort of the ride. The greens of undamaged trees appeared particularly vivid, as if throbbing within. Time slowed and accelerated unpredictably.

In the cover of an old, umbrous wood the truck stopped briefly to let the men stretch their jarred muscles and bones. Heck opened a C-ration—a can of compressed cold, greasy, unrecognizable meat and filler—but he could hardly swallow the first mouthful. He threw away what remained and ate instead a chemical-flavored D-bar.

They started again with a lurch. As they came nearer the front they began to see horses that had not been dead long enough to swell. And beside the horses now lay men. A smashed panzer was still smoldering and leaking smoke. A naked, blood-encrusted, unlimbed torso hung in midair, tangled in the temporary telephone lines strung alongside the road. Two American soldiers stood beneath, and one of them held a wooden staff that had been perhaps the handle of a shovel or broom. It was too short, however, to dislodge the torso, and as these two men receded into the distance, one was climbing onto the shoulders of the other.

Shortly after, a lone Sherman stood beside the road with several men gathered around. Steam rose in fast unfurling billows from the open engine compartment while one man repeatedly swung a helmet overhead and down into the steam. Shadows grew rapidly across the fields and soon the sunset on the towering clouds behind them looked like Armageddon and it was as if they were fleeing the end of the world. Darkness settled in. Artillery now rumbled like a continuous thunder. Flashes of light appeared on the horizon. No one spoke. Heck took off his helmet and turned it in his hands and put it back on. The man beside him checked the action of his M-1. They passed several buildings that were burning hot enough to be felt inside the passing truck. A fat woman sat beside the road with her legs straight out, like a doll's, wailing.

At a crossroads amid open fields the truck stopped. They sat unmoving for what seemed a very long time, then started ahead at an agonizing, crawling pace. They stopped again, and once more, for no apparent reason. It seemed—in the darkness—this might go on forever. The truck accelerated, stopped, turned, at one point reversed—perhaps they were going in circles. Heck took the music box from his pocket and sat holding it in his lap, running his fingers along the edges.

"What's that?" said the man beside him. Heck looked down and saw that the metal of the box glimmered with faint blue edges in the dark. "A music box?"

In the dark Heck nodded. He moved to return it to his pocket.

"Play it, why don't you?" said his neighbor. "Go ahead."

Heck wound it and opened the lid. The notes moved within

the random noise of the wind, the artillery, and the truck's creaking and shuddering so that sometimes the music was submerged and sometimes several notes could be heard quite clearly. It sounded extraordinarily beautiful to Heck. When the music stopped, the soldier beside him took the box from him, wound it again, and held it to his ear. When he handed it back, Heck allowed the last, slowing notes to play out, then closed the box and returned it to his pocket.

A minute later the man beside him asked, "Are you afraid?" He spoke with a sympathetic tone, but also rapidly—an easterner, Heck guessed.

Heck failed to respond. Pockets of orange light flickered on the horizon, and the corresponding percussion arrived several seconds after. An elbow nudged him and the question was repeated, "Are you afraid?"

The voice spoke softly, but even so Heck was not certain that others in the truck could not hear. He said, "No, I'm not."

"I am," said the voice, rising slightly in pitch. The truck shuddered through a rapid series of potholes. "I'm glad I am. As long as I'm afraid, I'm still alive." The body beside Heck shifted slightly. "How come you're not afraid?"

Heck felt irritated and at first he was not going to answer, but suddenly he conceded, in a rush, "I guess I am a little."

"Yeah?"

"I guess."

"Good. That means you're still alive too. I hope I stay afraid through this entire war, then go home afraid. I want many long years of fear after that, afraid for a wife, afraid for children—as long as I'm afraid for them, that means they're still alive too, because you don't feel afraid for someone who's already died, you just feel sad and sorry. Then at a ripe old age, still fearing death, I'll die. That makes sense, doesn't it?"

"Sure."

In truth, though, Heck was so clenched up with nervousness he could hardly follow his neighbor's line of thought. He glanced over at the man. All he could see were the eyes, which were large and protuberant, and the whites were a faint blue glowing all around the irises. They gave an impression of permanent startlement. "What's your name?" the voice asked.

"George Tilson. But people have been calling me Heck."

"Heck? That's a funny name."

"I guess."

"Don't be offended. My name is Anthony."

The truck made a sharp turn that evoked curses and forced everyone to clutch at their rifles and sent packs sliding over the floor. Gradually things and people were restored to their places. The truck's up and down and side to side had surpassed the point of causing simple soreness and had become a kind of torture. Heck accepted each new jolt with hatred. On top of this he might die tonight.

Anthony said, "You're still a little afraid?"

"Yes."

"Me too. I figure as long as we keep this up, we'll be fine."

Now, suddenly, artillery shells were landing not far away, and in their flickering light the silhouettes of a town could be seen, buildings dimly visible on either side of the road. The truck slowed to a crawling pace but did not stop, and the corporal jumped out of the cab and came to the back of the truck, saying like a rapid chant, "Out! Out! Out!" The men stood,

heaving up their packs. Heck was pushed out by the man behind him, and he flailed briefly in open space before hitting
cobblestones with his knee, hip, and shoulder. He scrambled to
get away before another soldier landed atop him. The truck
never fully stopped, was in fact accelerating before the last pair
of men had jumped out. Heck saw the others gathering and
started toward them, but the corporal bellowed, "Spread out!
Spread out! For God's sake, don't clump together!"

Heck ran into the dark, realized then that he could no
longer see anyone else, and reversed himself several paces. The
truck was gone. The corporal had a map in his hand and was
moving a cigarette lighter over it and muttering incomprehensibly. Heck crouched and pointed his M-1 into the night. Close-
set houses lined the street on either side, illuminated in flashes
by the impacts of artillery shells landing several blocks over.
The explosions were disorientingly loud, and he could feel the
shuddering of the earth. There was also, from somewhere
across town, the noise of sporadic rifle shots and the rattling of
machine guns firing and sometimes overlapping in a kind of
chorus.

The corporal stood and called out orders and they moved
off in single file, into the city, a string of cumbersome, laden figures hunched over their guns. "Spread out, spread out, damn
it," the corporal hissed, and they did, but a couple of minutes
later, Heck noticed, they were bunching up again. He didn't say
anything; it *felt* better to have someone nearby.

They moved through several blocks in this manner. The
corporal stopped at the corners and sometimes referred to a
map, then waved them on, with further cursing about their
spacing. "A single shell will wipe out every one of you useless

shits." Often in the darkness Heck could not see the man in front of him and he trooped forward blindly, his heart hammering.

A shot, loud, from somewhere nearby, was followed immediately by the noise of it striking the wall beside Heck. He spun away from the noise and fell over backward, his pack pulling him that way, and he landed on it, his spine arching uncomfortably. Another GI stepped on Heck's hand and disappeared. The first shot was followed by several more that moved along the wall over Heck, then suddenly dropped and began to ping and whistle askance off the street, throwing sparks where they skipped off the cobbles. Heck struggled to right himself, his thoughts flashing in erratic and incoherent panic. Another soldier tripped on him, fell, cursed, got up, and ran ahead. Heck had to roll sideways to get off his back before he could leverage himself upright again. Shots continued to ring out at confusing, arrhythmic intervals, whining hideously off the street and buildings. Ahead one of the GIs was returning fire and someone was shouting, but Heck couldn't understand the words.

He ran forward, blind in the night. He tripped, got up, ran on. A bullet skipped, sparking just before his feet. Suddenly something had Heck around the chest and he was pulled sideways; he nearly fell again. He brought his arms up in a violent attempt to free himself. "Jesus Christ, calm down," said the corporal's voice in his ear. He held on to Heck's shoulders until Heck slumped in acquiescence. "Keep moving forward," said the corporal, "and keep to cover, but stay calm, maintain distance to the man ahead. That sniper can't see us any better than we can see him. So don't fucking panic." The corporal let go and Heck, although still electric with adrenaline and occupied with jumpy, fearful thoughts, had himself under better control. Dimly ahead along the street he could discern a figure moving away; he followed it.

They moved cautiously between looming, three-story buildings with boarded windows, keeping to cover where they could and cowering every time the sniper fired again. The sniper was following them, or there was more than one sniper, or the same sniper had the supernatural ability to be in several positions at once. Heck could not understand how the sniper continued to fail to hit anyone, and as he crept ahead his thoughts ranged over the places he might at any moment be hit—arm, hand, leg, foot, hip, rib, neck, face, ear, elbow, shoulder, belly, spine, eye. There were so many possibilities. He presented a huge target. His entire body ached in an anticipatory tension. Traversing half a block in this way—with a horribly heightened sense of expectation and every movement and every sensible element of the surroundings given fearful, vicious attention—seemed to require a period of time longer than Heck's entire preceding life. Yet as he continued ahead, he also began to feel also a certain dim pride.

Then a new noise: a fluttering whistling with a rapid crescendo ended by a massive detonation. The building beside Heck lit and shook, dropping a cascade of bricks that broke into skittering fragments at his feet. Reflexively he fled in the opposite direction, but he had gone no more than a couple of paces before the building there erupted with an explosion. He stood in the middle of the street, gripping his useless rifle. The sniper was firing again. Several people were shouting. Another explosion illuminated a form that might have been the corporal, waving his hands in the air, and Heck ran toward him. Another shell crashed into the first building, and the entire wall along the street collapsed with a noise like the pounding of an enormous wave. A great foaming of dust welled up and Heck could see nothing—his eyes burned and filled with tears when he tried to open them. But he could understand the corporal's shouting now: "Dig in over there! Over there! Get off the God-damn street!" Heck stumbled into someone. His elbow was seized and he was turned and shoved. "That way!" Heck fell three times, and the third time his hands landed in soft, turned soil. He got up and moved ahead a little farther, then collapsed, fumbled the entrenching tool from his web belt, and began to dig blindly. The explosions continued but were at least behind him now, among the buildings. The noise was horrendous. He dug into the earth but hardly knew what he was doing. It was as if his conscious mind had crawled away into some corner from which it could cast out an occasional, fearful glance while his body operated under the command of instincts that Heck had not known existed.

Finally he had gouged a shallow hole into the earth and curled himself inside it. He wiped at the dirt and dust on his face and tugged at his helmet strap, elated by the fact of his survival. He had come under combat fire and he was still alive here in this wonderful dirt hole. He'd been frightened, but now he was okay. He was alive; it was a shocking and fabulous thing, to be alive.

But then the enemy artillery shells began to locate the field and land around him. The first blast threw a blanket of dirt over him and knocked him violently against the side of his shallow hole. Fear returned and consumed all other thoughts. Further blasts hurled him back and forth. The noise was like nothing he had ever experienced before, a noise such as might be used to herald the beginning of a terrible new world, and now, as he was bodily shaken and thrown by this wracking of the earth, there was no time, no memory, no future, no self, no control or sense beyond fear. He was reduced to the purest sensation of that single, awful fear.

Time passed; the artillery attack continued. Consciousness came again in the faint thought that he should have dug his hole deeper. He became aware that he was crying, in great sobs. He made no effort to control them. He could not move his legs. He discovered they were buried in thrown earth. He heard someone howling, a noise of pain. He clung fitfully to a tenuous understanding that he was still alive. He could determine this because he was afraid, and because he was afraid he was still alive and his body could not be completely shredded. Quickly, however, these notions became confused and he believed that only the dead could be afraid or that only the alive could exist in parts, and his panic and fear, though he would not have believed it possible, mounted higher. He screamed with his mouth full of earth and he squirmed, seeking reflexively to burrow and press himself somehow lower. He wanted utterly not to die and would have offered anything at all for the promise of life.

When the attack stopped, and Heck had lain without moving for some immeasurably long period, he carefully lifted his head. The howling he had heard earlier had ceased, and Heck was unsure now if he had imagined it or if it had even been himself he had heard. He examined minutely each of several barely visible piles of thrown earth and stone around him; then he began to slowly shift one of his hands free. But there was another explosion, and once again the shells were crashing. It was as if the respite had never occurred, and this convulsing earth and terror was all he had known or would know and there was no hope of an ending just as there had never been a beginning for this elemental, anguished noise and burning of the mind was all that had ever been.

The barrage paused again and eventually Heck could hear his own sobbing—it was now the loudest noise to be heard. Gradually he gained control over it. He lay still a while longer, then looked cautiously around, once again scrutinizing everything for signs of life or animosity. He spit the dirt from his mouth. The belt of fear around his chest began to loosen. Suddenly something heavy landed beside him, tumbling halfway into his hole, and Heck nearly screamed but restrained himself enough to reduce the noise to a terrified moan.

A face lay just beside his. It was Anthony's face, Anthony with the white-rimmed, startled eyes. Anthony was shouting. He did not seem to recognize Heck. "—move out. That way." Anthony pointed with his chin. "Follow about thirty seconds behind me. Corporal thinks the snipers will be on us again." Then Anthony heaved himself out of the hole and vanished.

Heck felt around for his gun. He could not locate it on either side or beneath himself, but then he kicked something and was able to pull it up from where it lay under his feet and hug it to his chest. Holding the weapon provided a short surge of relief and he pressed the gun more tightly. Something smelled bad, and he realized that sometime during the bombardment he had loosed his bowels. He now had no idea at all how much time had passed since Anthony had said thirty seconds. He began to count down from fifteen.

He had reached six when the sniper's rifle cracked and Heck

heard the bullet bite into the earth, though how near or far away he could not tell. It seemed near. Now he had lost his count. He took his breathing under control again and wiped with his dirty hands at his dirty face and began counting downward from ten. He kept to the count and did his best to ignore the further shots of the sniper. He counted slowly, metering his breath, tense in the shoulders and thighs: "Two—one—" Then: "Go."

But he did not go. He curled and uncurled his toes but lay as before. Involuntarily he groaned. The sporadic sniper fire continued, the bullets beating into the earth with a sound like a fist into flesh, and Heck dared not even raise his head to look around. He breathed, breathed again, and still he had not moved.

In a condition of despair he began to count downward once again from ten. A brief hissing noise of descent and a brutal explosion announced a renewal of the artillery attack, and Heck felt again terror but also a tiny lilt of relief as he pressed himself to the earth and allowed himself to forget any idea of moving out of this hole.

The shells came down in a furious series, then continued in a desultory fashion for, it seemed, a very long time. Then came another of those deceptive respites, but this one went on until even the ringing in Heck's ears had dimmed to almost nothing. Still he waited with his face pressed to the ground. After some number of hours had passed he began to feel a warmth on him, which, he thought, could only be the heat of the newly risen sun.

He raised his head. There was no sun, but a wash of blue glowed in one quadrant of the sky. All around him the earth lay ripped, blasted, and savaged. It would be better, he thought, to move now in this half-light than to wait for full daylight, when the snipers could see him clearly.

He rose and moved in a crouch, proceeding from one hole to the next, trying always to keep low and covered, never feeling himself low enough or sufficiently covered. All of the holes he ducked into were empty, which surprised him. He had assumed that the others were still here, and he was confused. He risked very briefly standing erect and looking around. He could not see anyone.

He sprinted ahead to the next hole, and the next. Sliding into a particularly large excavation Heck saw, happily, that here, after all, was another GI, cowering in the bottom of the hole. The soldier was so huddled and afraid that Heck felt a repugnance. "Hey, it's okay," he said. "Did the others go? Do you know? Did they leave us?" The other GI did not answer, catatonic perhaps, with his arms pulled tightly around his face like a child. Heck moved down next to him and when he reached out to nudge him, his fingers sank through the man's ribs into a moist hole. Heck flinched away and looked at his hand in the pallid light: his fingers were covered in a dark substance. "Are you all right?" he said and reached to shake the man again, but stopped short, his bloodied fingers hovering over the man's shoulder. The man in his cowering position had not yet moved and the touch of his flesh had been cool. Heck turned away and rubbed his fingers violently against the earth and got out of the hole and ran.

That man was dead, he thought. That man was dead. And the feeling of his fingers sinking into the flesh came back to him. He wiped and beat his hand against his trousers as he ran.

He came to the end of the field. There was a ditch and,

shortly beyond, a brick wall eight or ten feet high. Sitting at the muddy bottom of the ditch he felt well hidden. He discovered he had lost his helmet. He felt no desire to go looking for it.

He began to rub his eye with his fist, but stopped suddenly and examined his hand. Traces of dried blood remained between the fingers. He scrubbed his fingers with some of the mud from the bottom of the ditch and rinsed them in a standing pool of brown water and wiped them against his shirt. With a clump of dead grass he did his best to clean out his pants where he had soiled them.

While the sun emerged and ascended he remained hunkered in the mud. He felt relatively sheltered, and any other alternative seemed less safe. Eventually even from his position within the ditch he could see the sun burning above him.

He heard, faintly, noises of growling and clanking. The sounds slowly grew louder, until they were unmistakably the diesel engine and clomping treads of a tank. As the noise approached, however, its origin seemed to shift, echoing off different buildings, causing him confusion as to which direction he should flee toward. He decided he would do best to stay hidden and hope they would pass by. After the disorder of the previous night and the pounding the Germans had given the town, he assumed that the enemy had retaken the territory—if it had ever been in American possession in any realistic sense at all— and not until the tank came into sight at the far end of the field with a large white star upon its turret did it occur to Heck that this might be friendly armor. He remained hidden, watching, bothered by the idea that this might be a trick or that if these were Americans they might mistake him for the enemy but held primarily by an inchoate uncertainty that he did not question.

Behind the lead tank moved a squad of infantry, in American uniforms, and behind these followed two more tanks. He didn't see any of them look his way. The column passed by and out of sight, and he felt relieved when he seemed to be alone again.

The odors of phosphorous and cordite still hung in the air. He took a C-ration from his pack and ate quietly. It tasted horrible, but he ate it. Gnats swarmed in vague patterns over the field before him. Shots and occasional artillery exchanges could still be heard in the distance, but they sounded very far away and had nothing to do with him. In his mind he was still trying to assimilate the events of the night before. The sensation and the echo of his terror would not leave him, kept returning him to the darkness, the explosions and wrath, the sound of howling, Anthony shouting at him to move out.

He took the music box from his pocket and opened it and closed it, thinking vaguely of Claire. He smoked a series of cigarettes. Slowly an understanding of his actions came to him. Evidently he had waited too long after Anthony told him to move out. Probably he should have gone to talk to the Americans who went by with the tanks. Still, not until midafternoon did he feel sufficiently calmed to consider stepping into the open. Even the distant sound of artillery had stopped, although there still erupted, at unpredictable intervals, crackles of gunfire in town. It occurred to Heck, suddenly, that if he did not make an effort to find his unit he might be considered a deserter. This was an appalling thought and it startled him into motion. He closed his pack and settled it on his shoulders and, gripping his rifle tightly, ventured onto the field where the gnats moved.

He did not look carefully into every hole, but it appeared that the only casualty was the man he had stumbled on earlier.

Heck maneuvered around him and avoided looking at the body. He could still feel his fingers going into the dead man's side, and he glanced at his hand to be sure it was not wet with blood. He wondered if the screaming he had heard had come from that man. Maybe another man had been wounded and the others had helped him escape. Heck's sense of the events of the preceding night was vague, uneven. Only the memory of fear ran continuously through it, like a thread connecting otherwise discrete beads.

When he stepped out into the cobblestoned streets he found a town that had seemed much larger in the night. The blocks had been longer, the buildings taller. Much of the town was in fact destroyed, reduced to skeletons or simple rubble. Littered along the cobblestones were packs, gas masks, shell casings, a boot, a grenade—evidently a dud, although Heck did not go near enough to examine it. The smell of burning and char was in the air. Wisps of unenthusiastic smoke rose from smoldering buildings.

He progressed vaguely, moving in oblique directions, tacking like a ship into the wind. It was strange to see how a house could stand pristine, even its windows intact, immediately beside a house that had exploded, burned, and collapsed into its own foundation. He passed two burn-scarred tanks, one just behind the other, a naked blackened corpse extending from the turret hatch of the second, locked in a position of dragging itself away. It had a terrible quality of suppressed life, as if it might yet make a last inhuman effort. He left these behind and turned a corner and moved down a street where the houses were close-set and all of them had taken damage. He came to another building that had fallen into its cellar and across the rubble glimpsed someone moving in the next street. He stepped behind a corner. But he thought it might have been an American uniform he had seen. And now he heard American voices. Tears came to his eyes—he was surprised by the intensity of his relief. "Hello," he called, stepping forward, waving his arms, then more loudly, "Hello!" There were two men, he saw now. They turned to look at him, one leveling a rifle. Heck started gingerly forward across the ruins of the collapsed building between them. "Hi," he said.

"Who the hell are you?" called the one without the rifle. He had sergeant's stripes. His helmet was scorched black.

"I got lost," Heck said. "I don't know where the others have gone."

The one with the rifle muttered something. He lowered his gun but watched Heck skeptically. "All right, come on over," called the sergeant. "Maybe we can help you find your mama duck." Heck followed a long, thick wooden beam out across the fallen building, then stepped off the end of it, onto the frame of a fallen doorway, but under his weight the frame turned and there was nothing below. He fell, striking a sequence of hard, unseen objects, and landed on his knees in an ungainly way, twisted to one side. He felt like he had scratched his leg. "Oh, good Christ," said a voice above, not the sergeant's. Heck gasped to regain his breath. Dislodged debris rattled around him for several seconds. The sun penetrated the rubble in slivers and needles of light that swirled with dust. Heck slumped against the bricks and wood behind him.

The sergeant called, "You okay, kid?"

"I'm fine!"

"That wasn't pretty."

"I'm all right."

"Hold on to your socks. We'll fetch you out."

Heck felt embarrassed at the prospect of waiting for a rescue. He peered about. He might be able to climb up to the place where he had fallen in, but it looked precarious and could drop him again. Before him one wall had collapsed against another to form a narrow triangular opening. Possibly there would be some upward access through there. Above, the soldiers were laughing at something. Most likely him.

He began crawling forward, but soon regretted it. The situation reminded him of the cave in the cliff, and he thought of Claire and felt a guilty confusion. He could not see where he was putting his hands, and probing blindly forward he anticipated, again and again, the sensation of his fingers sinking into a dead man's mortal wound. The scratch on his leg bothered him. Then, however, he saw light ahead, and he moved faster and faster toward it.

As he crawled out into the light, he saw before him a staircase, only half-collapsed, which he could easily climb to the street level. It was a very happy surprise. He stood and straightened his shoulders and marched up to the street. He found himself behind the two soldiers he had been talking to—they were moving cautiously across the rubble toward the place where Heck had fallen in. The sergeant, in the lead, had picked up a long piece of wood that he used to probe the rubble. Heck took a moment to gather himself before calling, "Hey. I'm here."

The two turned and stared. There was a silence. Heck, discomforted, said, "I crawled out."

The sergeant laughed. The man with the rifle grimaced. The sergeant threw his stick aside, and they both started back. When they were nearer, Heck saw that they were filthy, arms and faces gray with grime. The one with the rifle had dark hair and a cauliflower ear and he finally slung his weapon over his shoulder. The sergeant had perhaps a week's beard and light blue eyes that made a striking contrast against the dirty flesh around them. The top of his helmet was blackened as if it had been turned over and used for a pot. Into the front of his belt was tucked a German Luger. His boots were crusted with what looked like dried blood. "So you think you're lost?" he said. "Who are you with?"

"Twenty-eighth Division, sir. One hundred and ninth Infantry. But I never found them."

"You're a replacement?"

"Yes sir."

"Well, you found your division. We're Twenty-eighth Division, Hundred and tenth Infantry. Your unit's ahead, crossed the river last night. You're a fucking mess, aren't you. Is that your blood?"

Heck peered down at himself, his arms, hands, stomach. He was dirty, but he didn't see blood until the sergeant gestured with the toe of his boot at Heck's shin: oozing through the grime on his pants was a glistening dark redness between the knee and ankle of his left leg. Heck bent and tugged his pant leg up. His leg was split open by a gash some six inches long. He touched the wound with his fingers—it was an inch or an inch and a half deep. The sight seemed unreal to Heck, as though this were somehow someone else's leg; he had never seen such a leg attached to himself before. He couldn't think how it had happened, unless he had hit something when he'd fallen a moment before. The cloth of his pants wasn't even torn, and he still didn't feel any more pain than he would if he had scratched himself on a thorn.

"Looks like you'll be headed straight back," said the sergeant. "Congratulations."

"Sir?"

"It hurt?" asked the sergeant.

"No, sir, actually."

"I bet it will soon enough." He produced a large, stained handkerchief from his pocket and tied it around Heck's leg. "Come on, let's get a medic to look at you. Keep your head down as we're moving. We're still trying to smoke out a sniper or two down this way." He put an arm around Heck's shoulders and led him down the street several blocks and around a corner to where an empty jeep stood parked in a shadowed alley. A sudden explosion caused Heck to flinch. Black smoke curled out of a broken window frame a block down the street. "Grenade," the sergeant commented. "Hopefully got him." A moment later a series of rifle shots echoed along the street, and the sergeant nodded in satisfaction. He helped Heck into the jeep's passenger seat. "Wait here. Find cover if you think it necessary."

Then he left.

Heck waited nervously. His hands trembled. He sat on them and put his injured leg up on the dash. He waited half an hour or so before a medic with a red cross on his helmet came and untied the handkerchief and looked at the wound. "You're lucky you didn't slice any muscle. How'd you do it?"

"I fell."

"Cut yourself on something?"

"I guess. I didn't really notice."

"That can happen when the adrenaline is up."

"Still doesn't feel like much."

"You're lucky." The medic tightly rewrapped the wound
with clean bandages, then walked on down the street, lighting a
cigarette as he went.

Over the next couple of hours, two more men arrived. One
had had his foot run over by a truck. The other had sliced his
hand open with a gilt silver-and-gold Nazi dagger while cutting
potatoes for lunch. He was nonetheless very pleased with the
dagger and showed it around. He said he'd found it strapped
to the ankle of a pair of kraut legs—torso, head, and arms
nowhere to be seen. "Pays to check everything," he said.

"Where are we at anyway?" Heck asked.

"Elbeuf. Scenic, fucked-up Elbeuf, on the scenic fucking
River Seine."

The man whose foot had been run over took out a package
of Life Savers candies and shared them around.

Dusk was obscuring the sky by the time their driver arrived.
He glanced at the three bandaged men with an expression of
distant curiosity. "Hang on," he said.

They jolted through several miles of twilight countryside
and scenes alternately serene and war-blasted. With each jolt in
the road the man with the crushed foot added a complaint to a
long muttered monologue. They passed haltingly down what
appeared to be an oxcart path. The sun vanished entirely. Heck
had difficulty comprehending that an entire night and day had
passed, a night and day in which he had been shelled, shot at,
gotten lost, somehow gotten himself wounded, and now was
being sent back again. They skirted scattered farms. The moon
rose. Heck touched the silver of the music box in his pocket. On

a dirt road through a wood they drove at high speed with only glimmers of moonlight to guide the way and ahead they could hear shouting and trucks.

They burst from the woods into a clearing and a scene of pandemonium. The driver braked and said, "This is the medical post. Here we are." He looked at his wounded passengers as if he expected them to get out, which, dazed, they did.

A house was burning, casting everything in a quavering and uncertain light and sketching long black unsteady shadows over the ground. Someone was shouting about *a spy, a saboteur.* Trucks and jeeps roared away while others arrived. Men ran around, others limped, and some moved, supporting each other. More than a dozen men lay on the ground, on stretchers; several were screaming. The fire was rapidly consuming a corner of a large farmhouse, and it was spreading. Occasionally someone threw an ineffectual bucket of water at it. More men on stretchers were being passed hurriedly out a window of the house. The shadows of men and trucks and jeeps wobbled and leaped against the faint silver forms of the trees at the edge of the lawn. Smoke spilled upward from the flames, which were now moving over the roof. The heat pressed against Heck in waves. Someone yelled, "Grenade! Grenade!" and there was a general, frantic scattering away, then a muffled explosion. The frenzy renewed and an officer began shouting, "Who the fuck put a grenade in there? What the fuck are you people doing?" A pair of scrawny, bleating sheep wandered among the men lying on the lawn. The screams of the wounded were horrible. Much of the running around seemed to be without purpose, and even the ambulatory wounded hobbled around in senseless agitation, as though no one could bear to be stationary amid the excitement. But they were being slowly gathered into the trucks, and a part of what was going on, Heck now saw, was that a poorly organized bucket brigade was trying to carry water to the fire. People were running forward and back, handing empty and full buckets to one another—many of the buckets were actually upturned helmets. Meanwhile the trucks cut through the lawn, leaving long muddy gouges in the grass, and a stuck jeep spun its wheels, flinging mud over several of the wounded, who screamed invectives. A sudden wind fanned the flames to a roar and swirled a blanket of smoke around Heck that blinded him and set him coughing. When he had blinked his eyes clear, the jeep and the men he had arrived with had vanished.

Within all the confusion he noticed one man, small and prim-looking, who seemed relatively calm. He was a medical officer, moving methodically between the men on the ground, talking with them, checking pulses, examining wounds. Heck limped over and caught his arm. The medical officer shook Heck away irritably and moved to another stretcher. "What's happening?" Heck asked, trailing after him.

The officer crouched over a man with his feet wrapped in so many bandages that he appeared to have volleyballs at the ends of his legs. Without looking up the officer said, "It wasn't any Goddamn saboteur. I'll tell you that. Overheated stove. I warned them."

"What should I do?"

"You're wounded?"

"I guess so. Yes."

"Get on that truck over there." The medical officer gestured vaguely and turned back to the man with the bandaged feet.

There were several trucks, arriving, leaving, parked. Heck

started toward a pair of trucks stopped side by side that appeared to be taking on wounded soldiers. But before he got there a man with wild hair and smudges of soot on his face handed him a bucket and ran off. Heck, in surprise, looked into the bucket. It was empty. He trotted with it to the hand pump and gave it to someone there, who exchanged it for a helmet full of water, which Heck carried over toward the fire and handed to someone, who gave him an empty one in return, and so this went on. Heck soon lost track of how many helmets and buckets he had carried forward and back. His injured leg began to throb painfully with each step, but the pain seemed of little consequence and he continued carrying water despite the fact that the bucket brigade was obviously having a negligible effect on the fire and it seemed that everyone in the house had now been evacuated.

Suddenly someone gripped Heck by the shoulder and spun him around. It was the thin little medical officer he had spoken to earlier, and Heck sloshed half a bucket of water over him. The officer yelled, "The hell are you doing?" He took the bucket from Heck's hands. "Let it burn. That's the last truck. Get out of here."

In the dark in the back of the truck Heck could see little of his companions. A pair of men on stretchers were slung up along one side. Others sat on the floor or on a bench along the opposite side. Heck pressed himself into a place between two warm, stinking bodies on the floor. The truck lurched forward, back, then forward again. Cold notes of wind hissed through the seams of the canvas shell around them.

The remainder of the night passed in a discomfort of bumping and pitching. Groans surrounded him, but quieted over time. Eventually Heck sensed more light, and peering out the back of the truck he saw a red sun coming up behind them. How the others could doze and sleep through the violence of the ride Heck did not understand. They were a filthy, mangled lot, and Heck had to suppose he looked no better himself. But they were moving away from the fighting, and recalling this created an irrepressible, lifting relief.

3.

A PRETTY NURSE WITH BLOODSHOT EYES ESCORTED HECK INTO a large brick warehouse. Its great open space had been converted into a hospital with rooms separated by curtains and crude wooden walls. In each room eight to a dozen men rested on narrow beds arranged with just enough passage between them for doctors and nurses to perform their duties. From where Heck was placed he could reach in either direction and touch the shoulder of a neighbor. The warehouse ceiling soared high over the makeshift walls of the hospital, so every sound echoed in that high open dim space and the disquiet of suffering resonated as if in a cathedral. Nonetheless, Heck had hardly slept in the past two nights and now he slept.

He was woken by a doctor with an enormous, block-shaped head. He gave Heck's leg a cursory inspection, talked through a drooping, unruly mustache. "Who sent you here? This should have been taken care of at the unit aid station. They should have put a few sutures in this and bandaged it and kicked you back toward the krauts. I don't want you here taking up a bed with a scrape like that."

"Yes sir," Heck said. "The station was on fire, sir."

"Nothing else wrong with you? No trench foot? No pain in your kidneys? Headaches? No combat fatigue?"

"No sir."

The doctor snorted, horselike, and made a note on his clipboard.

Again Heck slept. He was woken by an orderly peeling the bandage off his leg. Seeing him awake, the orderly said, "How'd you do this?"

"I don't know. I think I just fell down."

The orderly laughed. "Well, you're a lucky one. Put a few stitches in there, watch you a little while to make sure there's no infection, and get you back into the Grand Tour. How's that sound?"

"All right," Heck said, although he felt small desire to be in fighting shape again. The shots of anesthetic put in before the stitches turned out to be the most painful aspect of his wounding. The stitches were sewn in where he lay.

He remained for two nights in the hospital ward, and he observed that most surgeries were conducted in a separate, curtained room, and the sallow-eyed men around him who were carried there returned bearing long swaths of sutures across purpled flesh or returned without a part of themselves or returned not at all. Heck soon felt absurd and embarrassed to be lying on his bed with his meager, nearly painless injury while here and in the thinly walled spaces around him lay men who had lost limbs, whose several orifices would not stop bleeding, who ground their teeth as if eager to be rid of them, or who lay so still and pale that Heck would have thought they were dead if the nurses and doctors had not continued to come by and tend to them.

He contemplated his behavior in Elbeuf with unhappiness. Even now he could not allow himself to think directly of the time spent in that foxhole under the bombardment because the fear began to return over him and his muscles began to tremble. In angry moments he did not feel responsible for his own actions: he had hoped to do the right thing, but his efforts had been superseded by forces beyond his control. And yet he was often overwhelmed by a sense of shame at his cowardice, and he could only lie suffering beneath this feeling like piled stones.

It was a relief when he was ordered out of the hospital, into an arrangement of tents nearby holding those deemed ready for reassignment. The tents were drafty and set in ankle-deep mud that one traversed on wooden planks laid out in somewhat haphazard paths, but still Heck preferred this to the warehouse with its inventory of the dying and the maimed. Here at last he could see sunlight again. Here, although he shared his tent with seven others, he could at least sleep without the regular interruption of screams. He walked already with only a very slight limp and hardly any discomfort. And again he found himself with long openings of unsupervised hours.

Whenever someone asked how he had received the wound he said, "I don't know" and left it at that. He found that the other soldiers did not press him. He supposed they imagined some horrible, unspeakable experience, and he did not mind such a misunderstanding so long as it caused the questioning to end.

There really did not seem to be any reason why he could not

go back to the front. His stitches had closed the wound and it had scabbed over and he had regained complete mobility, more or less. But he received no orders, and Heck was reluctant to seek an explanation or to remind anyone of his presence, although he felt he should and at times even decided he would but then put it off. Within him, the desire on the one hand to redeem his sense of honor conflicted with the still dense memory of his fear. Between these he was suspended in a state that looked like passivity. Also, his thoughts often returned to Claire and the events in the cave. He experienced the physical sensations again and ventured toward how it would have been if they had gone on to consummation. He created entanglements of memory and fantasy so vivid that an outside noise would startle him, breathless, from the reverie.

He considered scenarios by which he might meet Claire again one day. He might marry her, teach her English, move with her back to the States. He entertained the idea that he was in love with her. Then the tragic fact that he would likely never see again the girl that he was in love with consumed him and he imagined that once the war ended he might spend the rest of his days wandering up and down France, searching with only the faintest sense of hope, the loss of his great love heavy in him.

What came back most vividly and often was the feel of her skin under his fingers, that smooth warmth, but occasionally now that memory shifted terrifyingly, especially when he lay nearly asleep, to the feel of the dead man in Elbeuf. In the horrible moment of that shift he could believe he had found her wounded, that she was dead, that he had killed her.

Even more quiet than Heck was the boy on the cot beside him.

One of the others mentioned in passing that the boy's name was Quentin. Quentin could not have been more than eighteen years old, and if someone had told Heck that Quentin was fifteen, Heck would have believed it. Thin and small, with pale blond hair and smooth translucent skin that showed all the blue veins beneath, Quentin spent most of his time writing letters and nursing between his long thin fingers a cigarette, rarely drawing on it. Often the cigarette would burn all the way down before he inhaled once off the stub, then ground it out and lit another.

Heck was unsettled by Quentin's quiet, although in truth it merely hung in equipoise with his own. When he saw that Quentin had, at last, run out of cigarettes, he offered one of his own. Quentin hesitated, as if accepting it would signify the acceptance of a burden. Finally he reached and took it. "Thank you," he said. He presented a meekness that was somehow not quite believable. He drew on the cigarette and positioned it carefully in his fingers. He looked round the tent before saying, "Thank you. What is your name?"

"George Tilson. But they called me Heck when I joined the army." It occurred to Heck that he liked this name, that he carried it before himself and insisted on it. It seemed to distinguish this person he had become from his past, pre-army self.

Quentin weighed things a moment. He admitted, softly, "That's a funny nickname."

"It's because I don't swear."

Quentin laughed. "You won't say *fuck*?" He glanced around before adding, "Fuck, everyone fucking says *fuck* here."

"I promised my mother, when I was little. And now she is dead."

Quentin looked away and back, twice, dartingly. "I'm sorry."

The conversation subsided. Across from them, two men played cards over a cot, using cigarettes for stakes and both smoking hard and fast enough to rapidly dwindle the stakes. One occasionally accused the other of cheating in a tone that meant he didn't mean it.

Quentin touched Heck on the shoulder. Blushing, he said, "I fell, getting off the truck, fell and hurt my ankle." He spoke low and confessionally. "Getting off to pee."

Heck told how he had fallen in the rubble of a building and Quentin nodded sympathetically. Outside, trucks could be heard moving and someone was elaborately cursing the mud and from the direction of the mess area came the metallic crashing of a dropped pile of steel dishes and pans—and the card player who had been accused of cheating fell heavily to the ground and slid under a cot and pawed at the ground and moaned.

Heck thought the man had heard shells or bombs coming, and he nearly rolled out of his cot and to the ground himself. But the other card player stared incredulously, and Heck realized that all the man had heard was the noise of the pans. The sound of the man's low, breathy simpering and the scrape of his fingers occupied the entire space of the tent. He was nearly invisible under his cot, but the cot itself lifted and fell like a large, heaving animal. His feet could be seen; he was barefoot.

Finally Quentin set his cigarette into the can he was using for an ashtray and walked over softly, almost on tiptoe, and bent to touch the man on the shoulder. "Hey, fella," he said. "It's okay. It was just some pans." Quentin tugged gently, and the man allowed himself to be drawn out. His hands were trembling but he smiled. He looked around smiling and sat on the end of his cot. "You all right?" Quentin asked. The man nodded. He gazed toward Heck, but Heck could see that the man did not see anything.

The other card player gathered up the cards. After a few minutes the barefoot man announced loudly, "I'd dropped something. I was looking for it."

No one commented. He was still staring in that way of not-seeing.

Heck stood and pulled on his coat and left the tent. He had to walk a long time before he could think of things other than that stare.

The barefoot soldier was gone the next day. A slow but steady circulation of men were assigned to the tent, then on to their units, creating a routine in and out of bags and equipment, rounds of introductions and good-byes. There was a sense of pressure in the air, as if dramatic weather were always imminent. Some of the men drank outrageously in town and were to be seen lurching about. Most, in their anxious boredom, attempted patience and resignation. One of the men in Heck's tent had stolen a radio, and, when he could run a cable to a generator, they listened to the BBC and the news of the front. The news was very good, and some said Berlin could be taken by Christmas. Heck had trouble imagining Christmas. He smoked a lot. He went into town each day and strolled the streets. He was familiar with brick streets at home but cobblestones were a novelty to him, and they provided welcome relief from the mud. The houses seemed small. It was very pleasant to meander around and peer into the windows of the bakery and the sweets shop, to watch the women pin up their laundry, the children playing games, the men loading coal bins in preparation for winter. The war in its inscrutable mercy had bypassed this town, and most of the people here were pleasant toward the Americans. Heck avoided the raucous cafés where many of the soldiers passed time, and the nearby house where, it was generally known, a GI could find a certain kind of woman. Heck began to enjoy listening to the French talking; he did not understand any of it, but it sounded to him like a pretty language, such as might be exchanged between birds. The town's children had learned to ask, in English, "Any gum, chum?" He acquired a black rubber hooded poncho and walked even when it rained, and although his boots, socks, pant legs, and bandage became soaked he little minded. In the rain the streets were almost entirely abandoned to his possession. He purchased a pipe and experimented with it for a day, but he could not keep the bowl lit without drawing on it hard and often, so that the tobacco was quickly burned out and his tongue felt scorched, and he reverted to cigarettes.

Within days routines had developed. When he paused to examine the offerings in the bakery window the same heavy-set woman inside always smiled and waved. A particular quartet of children were always the first to find him in the morning and as such were daily assured of fresh gum. He paused to examine the fountain in the center of town and tried to imagine what it would have looked like before the war, when it was fed with water. He imagined that on sunny days rainbows would play around it. There were three old men who sat in a row on a bench in the town square and argued constantly, with gnashing of teeth and gesticulations of exasperation and tremendous sighs of indignity. From the far side of the square Heck watched how arguments flowed between the three of them, sometimes these two against that one, sometimes another of the possible pairings, sometimes all three declaiming simultaneously and so exaggeratedly that there appeared to be no agreement between any of them on any subject on the face of the earth. In the early evening, phonograph music drifted from certain houses. Music seemed a marvel. Heck experienced occasionally a simple, powerful exaltation over the fact of being still alive. To be alive seemed the only fact that could matter, that he was breathing and warm and retained his limbs and senses.

He wondered if possibly the army had forgotten him entirely. The men in Heck's tent came and went and still he remained and he did not object. He was again in some vague military limbo, and he was beginning to understand that the army had many different kinds and places of limbo.

Quentin too remained, rarely leaving the tent except to eat. He tended to the tent's coal stove and to his letter writing. When Heck asked, Quentin said he was writing to his fiancée. He wrote on a steel clipboard that he had somehow begged or bartered out of the hospital, and whenever someone loomed near enough to read what he was writing, Quentin hunched over the clipboard and shielded the page with his hands. When someone tried to tease him about writing dirty to his girl, Quentin ignored it. He had a way of greeting people by looking away while smiling tentatively that reminded Heck of his own father.

Quentin seemed to have decided to regard Heck as a sort of fellow conspirator. Heck had taken the music box out to look at it for a moment before going to sleep when Quentin leaned over and asked, "Is it your mother's?" Heck shook his head.

Quentin wavered, then leaned nearer. "There is a girl? You're in love?" Heck started. Quentin grinned. "Yeah?"

They were quiet a minute.

"I've lost her," Heck said. "I don't know where she is."

"You have to find her."

"I don't know where. I don't even know where to look."

"What's important is to search." Quentin spoke with a rapid, hissing insistence that alarmed Heck. "You'll find her."

"I hardly know her." Heck put the music box away. "We don't even speak the same language. Her father is insane."

"Well, perhaps you're not in love."

Heck stared at his feet.

"Are you in love?"

Heck said nothing.

This seemed to give Quentin new confidence. He said happily, "Confused is a part of love. The confusion isn't important. What's important is what you do. If you search, it's love. If you don't search, it's not love. You're going to search?"

Suddenly Heck despised Quentin. "No," Heck said without looking around. "No. There's nowhere to search." But after a minute the bitter emotion was already fading, and he longed to take the music box out again.

The next day he began to try to write a letter to his father. But it all seemed so embarrassing—his foolish injury, this useless waiting. It seemed that from any words he wrote, any words at all, shame would ooze like blood from razor-cut flesh. He rolled over toward Quentin. "Hey."

Quentin was finishing his day's letter packet, folding it and wedging it into an envelope. "Yes?" he said, without looking up.

"What should I write to my dad?"

Quentin shrugged.

"Well, what is all this that you write to your fiancée?"

"I tell her how much I love her."

Heck wrote, "Dear Dad." He stared at this a minute. He said, "Okay, but what else?"

"The weather, the food."

Heck couldn't imagine that his father would care about these things. He wrote, "I'm doing all right. Little action." After a moment he added a bald lie: "But they keep me busy." He capped his pen and set it aside. To Quentin he said, "Do you have a picture of her?"

"A picture?"

"Sure."

Quentin looked away and did not answer. He sealed his envelope and put it into a canvas rucksack under his cot. Heck watched him a moment, then frowned and lay back.

An hour passed and several of the men were already asleep when Quentin leaned over and whispered, "Heck."

Heck rolled to look at him. Quentin's Adam's apple dipped as he swallowed. The soft blue veins at his temples pulsed. Heck tried to picture Quentin fighting a war, killing men. It was not an impossible image, but it was awkward—it could be constructed only as collage, its parts in disproportion to one another. Quentin said, "She doesn't exist."

"She's not your fiancée?"

"She doesn't exist at all. I wish she did. I wish she did so bad that I can see her, I can hear how she talks, I know what she does all day. I know what she smells like and what her favorite foods are and the kinds of clothes she wears. I know how she would write her letters back to me. She has a lot of questions, and I try to answer them all. But she doesn't exist. She's all made up."

"Quentin—"

"That's why you've got to find your girl, Heck. I've been thinking about this. You have a chance at someone real. She talks funny and her father's crazy, so what? So what? She loves you—why else would she give you that beautiful music box? That's why you've got to find her, Heck. She's a real girl. She loves you. You love her."

"Quentin, I—please."

Quentin looked around. "No," he whispered, apparently to himself, and shook his head. "No, of course not." After several seconds, however, he added, "But what else have I got? I haven't got a real girl. I'm in bad shape. I'm in lousy shape. You have a real girl, Heck. A real girl. You have to find her. Promise me you'll find her?"

Heck stared at him.

Quentin slumped. "I'm sorry. I'm sorry. Forget it."

It turned out to be very easy to go back. He was only forty miles from the Normandy beaches and the Channel waters, and he got a ride on a supply truck that was returning to Omaha Beach. The dead had been cleared from the roads and even some of the potholes had been filled. The driver whistled as he drove and he drove as if he knew nothing of death—Heck lost count of the number of times they were up on two wheels and came down again to four with a crash and a violent rocking of the truck. In a screaming of rubber they halted for a rangy-looking cow that stood in the middle of the road. They sat looking at the cow—the driver whistling "Take Me Out to the Ball

Game," Heck silent, the cow chewing cud—and several minutes passed before the cow moved listlessly away and the driver raced the engine and popped the clutch.

The driver began talking about his girlfriend back home. "She's got eyes like lanterns. One if by land, two if by sea—I'm coming back by sea. And her, you know, *melons,* they're big like her eyes. She complains, she says they're too big, can you imagine? Too big? I tell her they're just the right size for me. I'm a big guy; I got to have a big pair of melons."

Heck glanced over. The driver did not look like a particularly big man. He thought of Claire, the feel of her breasts. He said, "I prefer them smaller." Then he blushed.

The driver, however, didn't even look at him. He said, "Well, sure, some guys do." He began to whistle again.

Omaha was still crowded with fresh armor and mountains of supplies and general anarchy. The low, half-formed waves in the distance of the Channel were the color and shape of weals on flesh. Heck set away immediately for the château. He walked with the pulsing noise of the sea pacing him on the right, then turned and pushed inland. He passed rapidly through the little glade where the beehives stood. The hardwoods were dropping yellow and red leaves across the ground. The still-green pines looked a little odd, as if overly optimistic.

He reached the house and there was no movement, no sign of life. The door stood open and the doorway gaped blackly. In the mud outside were dog prints of various sizes.

Inside, his eyes adjusted slowly, parting the darkness in slow increments. It appeared as if no one had been here in months, or years. The little table was gone, as well as all the bedding, supplies, and even the garbage. A fine layer of dirt and dust lay undisturbed across the floor. He walked over to where he remembered the fire burning, but he could detect no trace of it: no ash, no blackening.

He looked up and above him floated the irregular hole in the ceiling that had vented the cooking smoke. In it the sky glowed with a clouded, parchment-colored light. It smelled here of animal feces and wood rot. It was strange to be here again—it had the quality of returning to a place not seen since childhood. He scuffed his foot in the dirt to mark for himself his physical existence. Then he stepped outside and stood in the relief of daylight and tried to think where they might have gone. But he had no idea; they could have gone anywhere.

He walked for a while unaware of his surroundings, thoughts shifting over his burdens of worry, what had happened to Claire and her family, how he would get back to the hospital, his cowardice, his fear. He pondered going back to the cave where she had taken him, but what would he do, crawl alone into the dark? He had no desire for the close darkness.

A hum of bees. He was in the clearing again. The noise of the bees was weaker and more sluggish than it had been when he was here with Claire. He stopped and stared at the hive she had opened. Then, slowly, he moved toward it.

He unlatched the front and peered in. He could see nothing but the seething movement of bees. With one hand he groped inward, trying to move his hand and fingers slowly and unthreateningly to feel in the corners, and he winced and muttered as he was stung once, twice, then three times. A fourth sting caused him to yank his hand out and stumble backward. His fingers were sticky and the places where he had been stung were already swelling. There had been nothing, nothing in there. The pain was intense.

He found a piece of paper in his pocket and, writing awkwardly with his left hand, printed on it, "Dear Claire, where are you? I love you. Iowa." He folded the paper and took out the music box and placed the note inside it. He was stung once more as he put the music box into the beehive and closed and latched it. Then he turned and sprinted through the woods toward the Channel.

Back at Omaha Beach he went into a medical tent and a nurse frowned over his hand and gave him a couple of aspirin and a moistened bandage. Then he wandered among the trucks. There were scores in various stages of arriving and departing, loading and unloading, idling, waiting in lines, maneuvering for position. He discovered the same driver who had brought him here. He looked at Heck's bandaged hand, looked at Heck. "Need a ride back?"

"Please," Heck said, nearly choking on the word and his gratitude.

4.

INTERMITTENT RAINS HAD FALLEN ALL DAY. THEY CAME AND went so slowly, and the trees and the tent flaps dripped so regularly into the brown standing water, that even when the rain paused it still seemed to be raining.

Heck stepped out to use the latrine and when he returned he found an envelope on his cot. On it was written only his name. No one else was in the tent. He lay on his cot with the envelope in his hands and the pinpoints of light that punctured the tent canvas seemed to be moving, twisting. Heck closed his eyes.

After a minute he sat upright and examined the envelope. The paper was thin and weak. He tore it open and found inside a single sheet of paper, folded once. He set the envelope aside and sat a moment with the paper in his hands, looking at it, wondering. With a movement of his thumbs, he flipped the page open. It said: "You God damned bastard."

Heck stared at the words, one after the next, forward, back. He closed the page, opened it again, closed it, until the shapes of the letters were etched into his brain. He put the page back into the envelope.

Quentin came in. "Letter from home?" he asked.

Heck nodded. Then he laughed. He did not know why he was laughing, but he laughed hard. Quentin stared at him. This was the most noise he had made in days.

Finally, gradually, the laughter dropped. Quentin asked, "You all right?"

"I'm fine," Heck said. He looked at the envelope and wondered, who had put this here. Which of the men had done this? It might have been any of them: to Heck, mired in his own problems, the men around him had all remained more or less indistinguishable, except for Quentin and the fellow who had cowered from the falling pans, but that one had been sent away a couple of weeks before. Heck didn't regard any of the others as particular friends or enemies. They came and went, from the hospital, to the front, faces, bodies filling cots; they became a blur and he gave them little heed. But one of them had noticed him. Perhaps this was just a joke. *You God damned bastard.* No, more likely someone had finally noticed that he was idling and wasting time here, that his wound, never serious, was now largely healed, that there was no discernable reason he should not be sent immediately back to the line to face the same risks that the others here had faced.

A red-haired boy with a white bulge of bandages taped against his right ear came into the tent, took something from the duffel bag under his cot, and left without glancing around. Men could be heard playing football in the mud outside—the quarterbacks shouted their snap counts, bodies smacked into bodies and into the mud. Occasionally the players broke into laughter. From the opposite direction came the tentative notes of someone testing a bugle. Boots struck the wooden boards laid over the muddy grounds with a cold dull impact followed by a faint suction. A jeep, far away, raced its engine as it spun in the mud, the engine whining higher and higher, as if the driver were determined to defeat the mud by sheer stubbornness. Then it stopped.

Heck wanted very badly to be rid of the envelope in his hand. He looked at the coal stove beside Quentin, who was loading a clean sheet of paper onto his clipboard. The stove was burning, but he didn't want to answer the question Quentin would sooner or later ask. He put on his coat and went out.

From the ranks of tents rose ranks of streaming smoke, released by improvised stovepipes built of rusting ductwork or cans welded end to end or, in one case, a 75mm gun barrel turned upright. The men playing football were extravagantly dirty and moved slowly in the chill, a race of mud-men engaged in strange ritual combat. Heck stood a moment on a muddy plank, touching lightly the envelope in his coat pocket. He looked at the tents and all the columns of rising smoke. He turned slowly. The bulk of the brick warehouse of the temporary hospital stood in the distance. There were several large woodstoves there. Heck stepped gingerly across a couple of planks, but the planks had become so interred in the filth that they offered little protection, and he soon gave up and set out directly across the mud.

He toiled across a churned and muddy field and by the time

he reached the warehouse he was heaving forward his sodden, filth-covered boots as if they were cloven hooves. A pair of ambulances stood near the door and some wounded were being unloaded. A stretcher went by bearing a cocoon of gauze—it was impossible to say whether anything human lay inside. A couple of orderlies were lounging by the door on a high-backed, ornately carved church bench. They were eating steaming soup from cans, gripping the hot metal awkwardly with pliers. A nurse hurried by, spattered from neck to knees with blood. One of the orderlies looked up as Heck knocked his boots clean. "What you want?" the orderly asked.

Heck had prepared for this question. He drew a pair of cigarette packs from his pocket for evidence. "Visiting my cousin."

"Brought him scags?" The orderly turned his attention back to his soup. He shifted his grip on his pliers, scraped with a spoon inside the can. "Stay away from the surgical areas."

Inside the only illumination came from occasional electric lights hung by long black wires from the ceiling. The odors of alcohol and cleaning chemicals were inadequate to obscure the vaporous presence of bile, pus, excrement, and human rot. The men in their beds either twisted and knotted themselves in the sheets or remained strangely still. Heck felt sorry for them all. He touched the envelope in his pocket and hurried toward the corner, where the nearest stove burned. A pile of wood as tall as Heck himself stood beside it. A spindly old man with gnarled fingers was tending the fire, and when he opened the stove door to fling a log inside, Heck strode up beside him, crumpling the envelope in his hand, and tossed it into the flames.

Moving away, he glanced back and saw the fire tender looking curiously after him. Heck abruptly turned down an aisle between long rows of wounded. He slowed and watched the faces as he walked. He told himself he had no reason to be surreptitious. He came to a soldier who looked lucid and calm, his legs wrapped in bandages, his left foot missing entirely. Heck said to him, offering the two packs of cigarettes, "Would you like some smokes?"

The wounded soldier's eyes neither blinked nor widened. "Sure." But he did not move to take the cigarettes, so Heck put them on the bed and hurried away in embarrassment.

He wanted to exit through a doorway opposite from the one he had entered. He moved rapidly down an aisle of wounded with, on one side then the other, the noise of pained breaths sliding past him. He reached the end of the aisle with a feeling of relief. Starting toward the door, he saw the doctor who had first assessed his injury in this same hospital. He hoped the doctor might have forgotten him, but already the man's big square head and thick dangling mustache had turned to Heck, and his features had tightened in recognition. "You're still here," he said.

Heck stopped. "Yes, sir."

The doctor had a clipboard in his hand and he gestured with it as if driving nails. "Why are you still here?"

"I've been awaiting reassignment. Sir."

"Why don't you go back to your unit?"

"No orders, sir."

"No orders."

"No, sir."

"How is that cut on your leg? Infected?"

"No, it's been all right. Sir."

"Haven't you made any inquiry as to your return to your unit?"

Heck had no answer. Seeing this, the doctor interrupted: "I'll see to it. What is your name?"

Heck thought of lying, but he remembered the note he had just burned, his daily sentiment of guilt. He said, "George Tilson, sir."

The doctor lifted a page on his clipboard, made a note, turned away.

When Heck stepped outside, even the thin light of the clouded sky seemed blinding. He wandered toward town in a state of aching anxiety.

As he walked through the streets the rain renewed itself. When occasionally he saw other people, they were huddled into the collars of their coats and under their hats and emerged out of the obscuring rain like headlong phantoms intent on tasks in the distance. Finally the wet and the cold began to penetrate into his consciousness, distracting him from his fears. He retraced his route back through town and past the warehouse.

Inside his tent it was warm and crowded and smelled of human filth and damp wool, burning coal and tobacco. Men glanced up briefly from conversations and card games and paperbacks. Everyone was here; all the cots were full. Quentin nodded at him. Heck arranged his things to dry as best he could and lay down. Later, while the rain still beat on the canvas of the tent as if in an infantile rage, two men asked him to join a cribbage game. As they played the two men debated, in startling detail, the relative physical merits of various pinup girls. That evening, when the cribbage had broken up and everyone else in the tent seemed to be writing letters, Heck lay worrying that whoever had addressed the note to him would do something as he slept. But he fell asleep anyway, and he dreamed of pinup girls on tractors in the fields of Iowa in summer. For some reason he was unable to go to them, or perhaps he only knew that they needed to work while the sun was up, but anyway it was pleasant to watch them. Eventually they began to maneuver the tractors through the patterns of a waltz. But then he saw Claire on one of the tractors, and she seemed to be looking for someone. Lust and fear and guilt and wonder arose and exiled him from sleep. By the time reveille sounded he had been lying awake for a couple of hours. He fully expected he would be put on a truck and sent back to the front this morning.

He was not. But Quentin's number was called. Quentin accepted the arrival of fate with bowed shoulders.

Heck sat on his cot watching Quentin gather his things. Quentin said, "I'm scared."

"You'll be all right. You'll take Berlin, then you'll go home and meet a pretty girl and get married. She'll be just like you knew she would be, and one day you'll show her all your letters, and she'll be amazed that you knew her before you had even met her."

"I have a bad feeling."

"I know." Heck could think of no further, truthful reassurance.

Quentin thrust the weight of his letters into his backpack.

"I'll probably be sent out tomorrow," Heck said, "and we'll meet up again in Berlin." He was straining desperately for words. "Hitler's living room. I'll see you there."

Quentin shouldered his pack and took up his rifle and looked at it like a thing he knew not how to dispose of.

Heck said, "I'm looking for her, Quentin. I'm trying to find her."

Quentin nodded. "That makes me glad. I knew you were in love." He offered a shy smile.

Heck walked with him to the truck. Quentin climbed in and they exchanged brief waves. Heck walked on toward town, wondering how many more people he would meet for a couple of days, then never see again.

The day was of such beauty that it seemed a mistake had been made. The air had warmed, and only one or two tiny, cottony clouds floated overhead.

The streets of town, to Heck's wonder, were a spectacle of color and movement, of voices and music. Beckoned by the weather, everyone was outside and the town square was full. There was a six-piece band, including accordion and dented tuba. The three old men on their bench argued spectacularly. The doors of the bakery were thrown open, and a yeasty aroma wafted out. Heck was still thinking of Quentin, however, and angrily resolved to himself that he would go back to the front and will himself forward. He knew now what to expect. He only needed to be disciplined enough to set aside reluctant instincts. Children careened in all directions, and soldiers of the various Allied armies strolled about gripping the necks of bottles and cussing merrily. Heck wandered out of the square and around a corner into one of the town's back alleys.

The buildings around the square were two and three stories tall, with steeply pitched roofs, built of brick or half-timbered and set tightly shoulder to shoulder. Some sagged or leaned with great age, and many needed paint. Nonetheless, they were evidently cared for and gathered to themselves a certain dignity.

In the alley, however, they displayed their shabby side—stained and unpainted walls, boarded windows, scattered broken brick, black burn markings. Heck stopped to look through an empty window into a large open space where the floorboards had been ripped up. Farther down the alley, a door opened and a woman set out a container full of garbage.

Immediately several fast-moving figures appeared—out of corners or from under stairwells. Some seemed to rise up out of the earth. All of them converged, shambling or loping, on the garbage can. They gathered in a small, gaunt, elbowing swarm, adults and children. Heck watched the little frenzied crowd from a distance. He started forward, then stopped. Among them was the boy, Ives—Claire's brother. He was struggling with two others for a bit of cloth that had fallen to the ground. He was the smallest of those involved, and he lost; a tall rangy old woman with the bearing of aristocracy won the little piece of cloth and skittered away. Ives turned to the garbage can again, but evidently the items of possible use had already been scavenged—the crowd was drifting apart. The boy peered into the garbage and sifted with his hand. Heck stepped into a shadowed doorway. The boy gave up and looked around. Heck could not see any disappointment in his expression, only a hardness of determination strange on a boy so young.

Ives trudged with his head bowed, pausing mechanically to look into other bins of already picked-over garbage. Heck hesitated, then followed. The alley ended against a creek of muddy water between steep embankments, and Ives put out his arms and ran toward it. He slowed slightly at the embankment's edge, then plunged down, out of sight. A moment later he popped up the other side. He turned right. Heck broke into a run. He reached the edge of the embankment and stopped. He glanced upstream and down, but the nearest bridge was a couple hundred yards away. The creek was swelled with rainwater and surprisingly wide. But Ives had made it across. The boy was now turning left into another street. Heck dropped with heavy steps down the embankment, looking at the churning waters, thinking it was too wide, that he could not possibly make it across. As he was planting his foot to make the leap he saw in the center of the waters a stone, dark and wet and nearly submerged, and he understood that this was how the boy had made it across. He twisted midstep to alter the direction of his movement and put his foot to the stone and skipped over. As he continued forward, upward, he found he had lost his momentum and he had to lean forward and grab at the soil with his hands for traction. After a short, muddy struggle he stood upright again, on flat ground, and sprinted to the right, then turned into the street where the boy had gone, beating his hands together to clean them and furious with himself and already aching with the anticipation of despair because there seemed little hope now that he could catch Ives. He should have approached the boy immediately, or called out to him before he vanished. And indeed the narrow street, which lay all in shadow despite the day's uncovered sun, was empty.

He searched up and down, gradually circling farther away. He had to slow to a walk. There was a heat behind his eyes and a tightening inside his gut. Ives could have led him to her, he thought, Claire.

He walked for a couple of hours. He returned to the town

square, where the band was still playing and the old men still argued. He sat on a low stone curb and watched. The soldiers drank and danced with the loose-jointed energy of puppies. Blue, white, and red bunting was strung over the shops. A second band set up across the square, to compete with the first.

Someone jostled Heck's shoulder. He looked around in annoyance, and here stood Ives, gazing expressionlessly at him, and it occurred to Heck for the first time that perhaps he was the one who had been followed.

"Ives, what are you doing here?" he asked. But the boy only smiled. Heck took from his pocket a couple of chocolate bars and offered them. Ives accepted them gravely and put them into a hidden place inside his shirt. Then he prattled out a torrent of French and made expansive hand gestures. He was jittery and bounced as he talked. The boy's foot seemed to have healed.

Then, with an exasperated roll of the eyes, Ives seized Heck's hand and dragged him into the crowded square. The little boy cried out and cursed in his high voice, gesturing with his free hand for people to clear the way. By now everyone in town had been drawn to the square, it seemed, for the streets beyond the cobblestones were deserted except for a few wandering drunks. Ives let go of Heck's hand and led him rapidly along. They again crossed the creek, on a low bridge. They passed a stone church, which, with dried flower arrangements on its steps and moss on its roof, possessed an air of reserve in the face of abandonment. Water sat in dull puddles on the street. Laughter drifted out an open window.

Albert was seated on a bench near the edge of town, his legs crossed in a pose of nonchalance. "Hello," he said. "How do you do?" He was dressed in an assemblage of rags, of which by far the cleanest and least battered element was the empty sleeve dangling at his side. The pocks on his cheeks appeared to have grown even deeper and more darkly purpled.

"Albert," Heck said. Albert's smile seemed strained, and it made Heck anxious. "Is your daughter here?" he said, looking around. Directly across the street from Albert was a small hotel and a flower shop. Behind Albert was a row of narrow little houses, their windows shuttered. Farther down the street the houses ended abruptly and the landscape opened into fields.

Albert said, "I did not really expect to see you again. I am glad we found you." He glanced across the street. "Maybe you should buy some flowers."

Heck said, "For her?" Albert smiled and stood.

Inside the flower shop, a gray-haired woman in dark glasses stood behind the counter. She was blind. Albert spoke to her in French, and she handed Heck a bundle of roses. Heck paid with a handful of coins, which the blind woman felt through one by one, then lifted her face and smiled at him. Outside Ives was leaping from the bench to the ground, ground to bench, bench to ground. Albert said, "Jumping around like a Cossack at a party." He adjusted the bouquet in the Heck's arms, then put his nose into one of the blooms.

Heck said, "Are we going now to see Claire? Where is she?"

Albert bent to kiss his son. The boy squirmed. Albert said, "A wonderful day, isn't it?"

Heck glanced at the sky, shifted the flowers in his hands. He felt slightly ridiculous with them. "You said you found me. How did you find me?"

"When she told me, I returned to the château, to see if you had returned. Your footprints were all over, and Claire found this. Why did you leave this?" Albert held out the music box.

He seemed to be offering it. Heck shifted the flowers and took it; its contours felt familiar under his fingers. He said, "How did you find me here?"

"You had returned. I knew you must have been injured. How could you have returned unless you were injured or dead? Or a deserter? If you were dead, you could not have gone to the château and left the music box. If you had been injured, you were likely to be here. In any event, the hospital was the first place to look."

Heck shook his head. "Take me to Claire, please. Is she all right?"

"You cannot see her yet. We must have reassurances first."

"Reassurances?" Heck glanced at Ives, and Ives stared back.

"But really I think perhaps you can guess what has occurred. Can you guess? Can you guess what you've done? Of course you can. I need not tell you."

"I can guess?"

"Yes."

"What?"

"Of course it will be obvious if you think on it. If you consider what you have done and its natural consequences."

Heck wondered if Albert knew somehow of his cowardice under the shelling in the nameless town. Or of how he had been dallying now in this temporary hospital. But he couldn't make sense of it, so he was silent, and watched Albert. He began to think Albert was toying with him in his confusion, which turned the confusion toward anger.

Albert said, "You understand."

"No."

"So. Then we must be very frank. You lay with my daughter, did you not?"

Heck stared a second at Albert, then flinched and looked away. She had told her father.

"Did you not?"

Heck nodded.

"So," said Albert, "as is the natural course and outcome to follow such events, my daughter is become pregnant with a child inside her and you, as father, are beholden to certain ancient responsibilities."

Heck, believing he had misheard or misunderstood, said, "What?"

Albert smiled in a gentle, avuncular manner and shook his head. "Let us not be coy. It is unnecessary. We are men. We are fellow soldiers. Surely you see now you have certain duties."

"She's *pregnant*?"

"Yes, precisely as I have said."

"I didn't do that. I couldn't have."

Albert wagged his hand in a gesture of deprecating dismissal. "Do not be stupid. I'm sure you are as aware of the basic facts of biology as I."

"No, I didn't."

"Maybe it is a surprise."

"No, no. You don't understand. We didn't do that."

Albert angled slightly forward and peered at Heck from under a lowering brow. "Of course you did. You told me yourself a moment ago."

Heck wondered if possibly he *had* gotten her pregnant. The

actuality of what had occurred and the repeated fantasies of what might have happened had become convolved in a way that caused him to doubt himself. Suddenly a thought struck him. He said, "Did you put that note on my bed?"

"I did, I did." Albert sighed theatrically, perhaps sardonically. "I should apologize for it. It was written in a moment of anger."

"I need to see her."

"Yes, but first I need to be sure that you understand your responsibilities now."

Heck backed away. This situation was impossible in every aspect. He needed space, solitude to think.

Albert stepped forward, closing the distance between them. "You will not run away from this. I will not allow it." He seized Heck by the collar and shook him. "You have had your pleasure. Now you must help her." He curled his arm, pulling Heck near enough to smell the wine on his breath. Albert's eyes were wide and staring, his pupils dilated. "Be decent, you bloody American shit." They were breathing on each other, Heck gazing with fear into the deep lines of Albert's face.

Then he raised his knee, hard, into Albert's groin. It was something he had once seen a girl do to a boy in grade school. It was effective—Albert let go and doubled over with a shocked gasp of pain.

Heck moved several steps away, watching as Albert tilted to the ground with his hand cupping his groin. The roses lay around him on the road; Heck had not been aware of dropping them. He still had the music box in his other hand. Albert's breaths came in hisses; his eyes were closed, then open, and he glared up at Heck.

Heck backed away, turned, and began walking. Behind him Albert said in a voice shallow with pain, "You coward." Heck walked on. More loudly Albert called, "You are a coward!" Suddenly Ives, who Heck had forgotten, sprinted past him and ahead, stopped, turned, and stood in the street with arms spread slightly like a gunfighter. Heck continued straight ahead, toward the boy. He decided he would accept without complaint or defense any punishment the boy could inflict. Ives held his ground, silent, grimacing, until Heck was only a step away. Then Albert called out, and Ives twisted to dodge from Heck's path, at the same time lifting his face. Heck felt a moisture strike him just below the eye. He did not, however, look back and did not reach up to wipe away the spittle until he had turned a corner.

He returned to his tent and lay abed the rest of the day. He seemed to dream without sleeping, for he was not tired and while he moved through dream he was simultaneously aware of the sounds and smells of reality. The next day he awoke expecting, again, to be sent toward the legions of Germany. Again it did not happen. He felt an uplift and he set off toward town, convinced that now he would find her.

However, the sky had clouded over, the temperature was low, the people in the street looked once more huddled and irritable, and Heck's sense of optimism rapidly declined. He stood for several minutes at the bench where he had found Albert, but no one was here. The flowers he had scattered over the street were gone. He went in to talk with the blind woman in the flower shop, but she could not understand his English, and he could not even pantomime for her. He walked the alleys looking for Ives, without success. In his mind he experimented with explanations or apologies or accusations he might offer Albert, none of them satisfactory. He spent much of the afternoon seated in the square, his hands slowly turning cold, then numb, watching for Ives or Albert. He thought he should not have kneed Albert in that way. He was bigger, younger, and stronger than Albert. He had, after all, two arms. He had acted in panic. *Coward.* He was a coward. It entered his mind that perhaps he should allow himself simply to be killed by the Germans.

He turned on his cot that night, unable to sleep. Whenever he neared that state of oblivion he seemed to find his hand inside the chest of a dead man and he woke with a start. In the morning he was told to grab his weapon and his bag, and he was put onto a truck going east.

5.

AT MIDDAY HECK'S TRUCK STOPPED IN A DEPOT BUSTLING WITH lines of vehicles and surrounded by barbed wire, antiaircraft batteries, and piles of refuse. They waited through a crawling line for fuel, then hurried through a town where brick dust swirled thickly off the ruins. Heck was the lone passenger in a truck that could accommodate twenty men. No explanation for his solitary condition had been offered, and Heck felt tired and hapless and had neither concentration nor patience to try to guess the reasons. After a couple of hours, when Heck next looked around, they had entered a density of tall pines. The pitching of the truck had become especially violent. They went on through pines for several miles, and the road became worse and worse. Suddenly the truck halted. The door of the cab creaked open. The driver peered at Heck over the tailgate, and his expression seemed to convey distaste for what he saw. He said, "Your stop."

Heck clambered out. He stood in a muddy rut with dense evergreen woods to either side. The truck had stopped in a minor widening of the road, just enough to allow the possibility of turning around. The driver was already climbing into the cab again. Trying to stall him, Heck said, "What do they call this place?"

"The Hürtgen Forest."

"You sure this is it? Where I should be?"

"Yup."

"There's no one here."

"Someone will meet you."

"When?"

"I don't know. Soon."

"I just wait here."

"You just wait here."

The engine roared and the driver put his head out the window. He frowned at Heck and his features tensed, as if he were resisting an emotion at the sight of Heck alone with his pack in his arms. "Best move," he said. "Unless you want a dirty shower."

Heck backed away. With much wheel spinning and flinging about of mud the truck worked itself around until it was pointed back down the road. With one last mucky flurry, it set off.

Heck dropped his pack at the base of a tree and, to avoid sitting in the mud, squatted on his haunches. The trees grew in long, close rows like ranks of soldiers or headstones, creating odd, flickering optical effects as Heck peered about. Overhead moved flat, shapeless clouds that granted only grudging opportunities to the sun. He sensed a damp, sharp cold lurking in the darkness underneath the trees. Somewhere in the far, far distance were artillery explosions, which Heck tried to believe bore no danger to himself. Time passed. He removed his helmet. His leg itched where he had been injured. A crow cawed and wheeled twice overhead, then settled into the branches of a tree across the road. The bird drew its wings in and observed Heck with one eye, then the other.

Heck extracted an egg-sized stone from the mud and stood and threw it at the crow. It was a long throw and nearly as high as it was long—the stone arced up and began down again. The crow saw it and lifted its wings, but too late, and to Heck's surprise and dismay the stone struck the crow with a soft *pok*. The crow dropped, following the stone downward through the pine boughs with a soft rustling noise.

A low voice behind Heck said, "First of all, don't throw shit around like that, you'll attract attention you don't want. Second, that was amazing."

Heck started and turned. The soldier he found was so unwashed and encrusted with earth that he might have just crawled out of the soil like a worm.

The soldier said, "Where are the rest of you?"

"Of me?"

"The others."

"I'm alone."

"I can see that. But what happened to the others?"

"There were no others. Just me."

"There weren't others that got killed somewhere?"

"No."

"Well, huh. Really? Do you want to fetch that crow?"

"What for?"

"I don't know. For eating? Just asking. Let's go. Stay close and quiet. The position, it's surrounded on three sides, so, stray off, you're going to end up in the shit. By the way, I'm Zeem."

"People call me Heck." But Zeem had already turned and started away. Heck shouldered his pack and jogged to catch up.

Zeem carried only his rifle and moved through the trees with a nimbleness that Heck, with his backpack, could not duplicate. He felt loud and clumsy and had to pause occasionally to disentangle a strap or sleeve from a low branch. His back grew sore from walking stooped under the pines. They followed a zigzagging path among the rows of trees and continued in this way for more than an hour. The forest appeared to grow increasingly dense, but this may have been only an illusion of the deepening gloom of the day's end. Then they passed through an area where many of the trees had been stripped of their branches, so that they looked like a congregation of battered telephone poles. Fallen foliage lay piled all across the ground. In places treetops and entire trees had come down or jutted at oblique angles. The smell of raw pine sap competed with the odor of cordite. Shortly after this, in a place where the trees were again dense and largely intact, Zeem stopped and waited for Heck. "Follow me," he whispered. "I'm going to go real fast. They got spotters on our position, and soon as they see anyone moving around they bring down a few shells. They hit the treetops and stuff goes all over the place. So, be undercover before they start banging. It'd be better if you had arrived at night. It's safer to move around then."

He set off at a run, and Heck lumbered after him. They

wove through the trees, the distance between himself and Zeem gradually widening, the pines tearing at clothing and flesh. Zeem had gotten as much as a hundred feet in front when he stopped, turned, and waved to Heck, then crouched and disappeared. Struggling for air, Heck ran on, reached the place where Zeem had vanished, and stood looking around. He saw nothing but trees and parts of trees. He felt a rapid expansion of panic in his chest. An explosion not far to his right threw him over into the mud. In a panic he struggled upright, and saw it— under a scatter of branches, a narrow gap down into the mud. Another explosion was followed by splinters and shrapnel falling with a noise like a heavy rain. Heck slithered forward, slipped off his backpack, and slid into the opening, a pig down a chute.

He landed face-first on the muddy floor of a dark space. The crashing of explosions continued, jolting the earth. He scrambled forward, bumped into someone's leg, stopped, lay still, then pushed himself up. Dimly he saw three figures. He was inside a hole perhaps five feet tall and eight feet square, lit by a few cracks of light in a log roof. No one spoke while the artillery bursts continued. Then the noise stopped, and still no one spoke. Heck's ears rang. His boots sank an inch into the muddy floor and created a nasty sucking noise as he tried to extract them. The others were seated on ration boxes, and Heck found another to sit on. One of the men fiddled with a radio.

Adjusting to the darkness, Heck watched the three vague figures before him gradually gather detail, becoming three filthy young men into whose faces a variety of bitter lines had been cast. Heck had the sickening feeling of having arrived here only by some unholy mistake. Zeem was nearest him, and gestured to another of the men—the one without the radio—and said, "This is the lieutenant."

He wore no officer's insignia. He was filthy and unshaven and cadaverous, his eyes rimmed red. Heck began to salute, but the lieutenant cut him off. "Don't ever do that here. Just get out of the habit. A sniper sees you do that, I'll be dead before I can say 'At ease.' "

The radioman looked up and added, "Then you'd be stuck in the salute. You'd look pretty dumb, I guess, standing there saluting a dead lieutenant."

The lieutenant nodded. "That's right. So no fucking salutes. Okay? Who are you?"

"Tilson, sir. George Tilson."

"Don't say 'sir' either. They might hear you."

The radioman put in, "I'm Obie." He smiled as if pleased by the sound of his name.

The lieutenant was looking through a notebook. "You said Tilson? Christ, we marked you AWOL weeks ago."

"I was in the hospital. I have my papers—"

"Doesn't matter, you're here now. We'll fix the paperwork. Ready to kill some krauts?"

"Yes, sir."

"Fuck! Don't use that word!"

"Yes," Heck said and stifled the following "sir" already on his lips. "All right. Sorry."

"Good. Keep your head down and maybe you'll get a chance. But it's really hard to kill krauts if you get killed first. That right, Zeem?"

"Extraordinarily difficult."

"Okay." The lieutenant looked at his hands, then shook his head as though the sight of his hands disgusted him. He said to Obie, "Who was it that lost his head yesterday?"

"Polanski?"

"Conlee's his buddy, right?"

"I think so."

The lieutenant looked at Heck. "You're going to join Conlee in his hole. Ask him to show you how not to get killed so you can kill some krauts. Conlee's done all right so far. Zeem, will you show him the hole?"

"I'll point it out."

"Good. And Tilson, try to find a way to dry your feet out once or twice a day. We're sending back too many men with trench foot. Stay buttoned down and keep your head together and you'll do fine."

For the moment, however, Zeem made no move toward the exit. Everyone sat listening to the radio fire staccato bursts of static. After a minute the lieutenant idly filled a ration can with mud, leveled off the top with a bayonet, and tested its weight in his hand. Heck said, "There was a man with me the first time I was sent out, Anthony. Is he here?"

The lieutenant said, "What's the name?"

"Anthony. He had kind of funny-looking eyes."

"I don't remember him," said the lieutenant.

Obie interjected, "He bought the farm."

"Who?"

"Anthony. It was before your time."

The lieutenant looked at Heck. "I'm sorry."

Another minute passed. "All right," Zeem said suddenly. He stood and led the way out. He ran ahead and Heck followed, dragging his backpack through the mud. Zeem stopped and pointed. "See that tree there? Broken off halfway up?"

"Yeah."

"Your hole is just below it. Hurry." Zeem turned and ran in the opposite direction.

Heck reached the tree, found a hole hidden under a few logs and a scattering of branches, and slipped inside as artillery shells began exploding again. His pack caught in the opening, and he tugged at it once, then left it. He found himself in a tight, muddy space, less than four feet high and just wide and long enough for two men to lie side by side. A helmetless GI squatted in the far corner, staring at Heck. His eyes were so deeply set that they were completely obscured in shadow, skull-like. In one large hand he gripped a cigarette. With the other he scratched in his beard. The artillery lifted after only a half dozen shells. The man with the cigarette said, "You're the one that's got the krauts all riled up."

"I couldn't get my backpack down," Heck said. "Through the hole."

"Food in it?"

"A little chocolate. Some rations."

"Take that out when it gets dark. The rest you're probably better off without. I left my pack behind the day I got off the truck. What's your name?"

"George Tilson. But people have been calling me Heck."

"Heck?"

"Heck."

"Heck—fuck. Heck." The shadowed eyes wrinkled a little, whether with mockery or merriment Heck was unsure. "Listen, Heck. I'm Conlee. Here's all the advice I can give you: when you need to move your bowels, when you absolutely can't help yourself, shit in your helmet. Maybe a K-ration box. Then throw it out that opening. Do not go outside to shit. Please."

Heck decided he could hold out for a while. "Yeah," he said. "All right."

"The last replacement I had insisted on going outside and died with his pants around his knees. Don't get too attached to anyone. Not me, not anyone. Certainly not the lieutenant, dear God—we go through a lieutenant a week. Don't get too close because they're probably going to wind up dead, and it probably won't be pretty, and it'll probably happen right in front of you. I'm sure as hell not going to get all chummy with you then waste time crying when a splinter of shrapnel gets you, and don't you do it for me. Best try not to get too attached to yourself either—that's the trick. If you can do that you're really in good shape, you'll be fine, one way or the other."

Then Conlee was silent. He finished his cigarette and lit another. Heck, crouching to stay out of the mud, began to hurt in the muscles and joints of his legs. He took off his helmet and sat on it.

Conlee, staring at Heck's thin hair, said, "How old are you?"

"Eighteen."

"Yeah? Me too." There passed a quiet moment in which, it seemed to Heck, each doubted the other's honesty. Then Conlee reached around behind himself and brought out a small cardboard box. "We've got a few of these little sterno heat blocks. You light them and kind of crouch on top of them, they'll warm your feet a little. Be careful they don't burn through the soles of your shoes."

"We just sleep here?" Heck said. "In the mud?"

Conlee stared at him a moment, then nodded.

The day-end wan illumination of their muddy pit very slowly dimmed, then was gone. Someone came by and dropped water and K-rations down. The cold and wet accumulated in Heck's muscles and began to make thrusts into his bones. Soon he was shivering uncontrollably.

From then on, the minutes and hours seemed to pass in clotted, desultory spasms, as if time were shambling forward with a great weight on its back and could advance only by effortful paroxysms. Every so often, preceded by a brief, fluttering noise, a few rounds of artillery exploded overhead. At one point there was rifle fire somewhere. Just before dawn, another round of K-rations came down.

For a time there was the light of day.

Heck began to understand that this was hell: a rainy woods, a place of mud and standing water and deep cold, made complete by the explosions that forced you to burrow into the muck and lie in it and be glad for it. Peering out the entrance to their hole he could see nothing that did not appear wretched and inauspicious. The damaged trees were stricken, ossified. When it rained the trees dripped, providing no protection. A fog was trapped or confused in the forest and dwelled there all day, at its thickest creating a white darkness. The mists seemed to absorb the night, and eventually night reconquered the mists, and in this fashion the idea of sunlight itself was erased.

Why this place was deemed of sufficient import to be held at the cost of men's lives, Heck did not understand. The Germans did not seem particularly interested in it, except insofar as there were Americans here who might be killed. In the night the lieutenant came around and stuck his head in the foxhole and said, "Morale is low. I know it is. Just try to keep your chin up." To which no reply was adequate, but habit gave forth a "Yes sir." "Stop that!" the lieutenant hissed. "And remember to dry your feet and socks every day."

Conlee said that some men deliberately allowed trench foot to set in, to escape this place.

Conlee brooded in a general silence that he broke with occasional curses and outbursts. He said, "This is shit. I'd rather charge into an army of ten thousand krauts, by myself, than suffer though this useless waiting with the krauts poaching on us. At least I could take out a couple with me. Here we're getting knocked off and we can't even shoot back."

Heck agreed, shivering.

He slept when he passed out from exhaustion. He awoke with no sense of how long he had been unconscious. He could not remember his dreams.

There were just the two meals a day, one after sundown, the other shortly before dawn. There was no hot food. A runner moving in the night brought the K- and C-rations that they ate cold with filthy fingers while squatting in the mud.

Thinking of what Conlee had said about how some men allowed trench foot to set in, Heck was tempted, and he waged a silent bitter battle inside himself, but he did his best to raise his feet out of the mud and switch his two pairs of socks, putting the off pair into his pants, where they might conceivably dry somewhat. He bitterly congratulated himself on a kind of bravery.

He and Conlee talked even less as time went on. Conlee seemed to dislike any conversation that might force him to regard Heck as more than a piece of mobile meat. Heck might have wanted to talk except that he was not in the habit of it and did not know how to begin. So they sat and lay side by side in the foxhole in silence.

When Heck managed to elide his situation for a moment, he thought of Claire and ran his fingers over her music box. He pondered in a kind of pained abstraction Albert's assertion that she was pregnant. Could it be true? He could not decide. If it was true, how had it happened? It was a mystery, but he felt a great pity for her and somehow it made his love for her even greater. He knew he would never see her again.

He hated the mud, which it seemed all the world was made of. He hated the cold, which never lifted but only modulated its degree of bitterness. It thrived in the damp and the dark and the mud and soaked into Heck so that he was uncertain if he could ever feel warm again; perhaps his skin might be warmed a little, but everything inside would remain soggy and chilled, like a swamp-soaked log. He hated also the fear that had soaked into him with the chill and which, like the chill, was never gone but only varied in degree of intensity.

Even in the hole, facedown in the mud under the logs, there was no real security. He learned that the incoming shells were preceded by a soft fluttering, gaining volume as they came down, and that the German artillery barrages moved in methodical patterns—he began to anticipate when the shells would land near him and when they would shift toward other positions. But though he might be able to anticipate the shells he could not stop them, and as the shells found their way down through the trees—which happened more often as the trees were gradually destroyed—eventually a direct hit would tear through the log roof and turn his foxhole into a small space where an explosion would have nothing to exert itself against but flesh. In addition to this was the menace of a German tank or infantry attack, and the snipers, and the terrifying likelihood of death every time one had to emerge from below ground.

After a bad shelling a roll call would go around, each fox-hole calling out that they were okay. Sometimes at the end Zeem called, "Now I want to take a poll. How many of you are still atheists?" An incorporeal laughter followed, hysterical and overlong.

Obie was occasionally heard to sing in a jaunty tone from wherever he lay in the mud:

"We're the Twenty-eighth men, and we're out to fight again
For the good old U.S.A. We're the guys who know
Where to strike the blow, and you'll know just why
After we say:
Roll on, Twenty-eighth, roll on, set the pace,
Hold the banners high, and raise the cry,
'We're off to Victory!'"

The silence that followed this seemed to Heck wholly impenetrable.

There were moments of pure hallucination. Heck was home again in bed with crickets and frogs crying in the night outside his window; he sat alone at a large table crowded with chicken and ham, cornbread and potatoes, thick vegetable stew and fresh salad, apple and cherry and pecan pies, cold ice cream, chilled milk—all of which he could smell but somehow could not touch; he was sledding down a long white hill with the hissing cold biting at his face; he was talking with a strange girl, explaining how sorry he was, how he loved her, and she understood every word; he was in a darkness with an anonymous woman touching every part of him, groaning.

Some nights he was posted to a watch position out in front of their location. He could see nothing, which at least assured him that the snipers also could not see him. But he would not have been able to see the entire German army if it was two arm lengths away. Nor was it clear to him what he should do if the entire German army did appear. Start shooting? Throw grenades? Run? Hide? Surrender? No one told him, and Heck assumed he was not supposed to ask. In the darkness certain noises cast Heck into a timeless gap where he waited for the sound of German steel sliding into his skin. He pointed his rifle at the noises he heard in the trees and brush but he never really considered pulling the trigger. He was too afraid of giving away his location. When he could hear distant shooting and artillery, he actually found the noise mildly comforting, evidence of a universe beyond the darkness before him and the imminence of his own death.

At the end of his shift he awoke the next man, then slid into the filth of his foxhole and, upon his bed of mud, without a thought of doing so, fell asleep.

Each day more wounded, ill, or dead were sent back. Meanwhile, somehow, Heck had become a veteran. He still had not fired his weapon.

Then they were suddenly ordered from their holes and began to march in the night. No one spoke. They seemed to be moving back toward the place where Heck had been dropped off, and he was relieved—they would get a respite, somewhere quiet. But soon they turned and marched farther into the woods. The trees blocked even the faint light of the moon in the clouded sky, and they had to move each with one hand on the pack of the man in front, and there were frequent stoppages, turnings, collisions, hisses issued to bring back men who had strayed off, painful encounters with branches. Heck lost all sense of bearing and location. He felt like one of a party of blind men.

When they came into a cleared firebreak, Obie turned and pointed out a thin white line running through the brush. "Follow the tape," he said softly. "That's the route. The engineers mark it through the mines." After a moment he chuckled and added, "Though, of course, sometimes the krauts sneak in and move the tape around."

They crossed the opening without incident and pressed again into the woods, forced to walk stooped, and often nearly doubled over, to pass under the low, tangled branches of the pines. Suddenly, at a point no different from any other that Heck could see, they were stopped and ordered to dig in. The GIs unfolded their little shovels and set to work. They had scant darkness left before dawn. Without a word, Conlee pulled him to one side and together they dug. Heck understood this as a kind of acceptance, and he felt moved with a deep gratitude and camaraderie.

The next night they had just started off again when a sudden explosion overhead was immediately followed by the whir and smack of high-speed metal and wood embedding into whatever they encountered. Someone began to scream. "Hug a tree!" Zeem yelled at him. "Stay under your helmet!" Heck ran for a tree. Another explosion; something tore at his arm. He reached a tree much too large to encircle with his arms and pressed himself against it. There were several more explosions in rapid succession. A second voice joined the first in screaming. Chunks of wood and shell fell in a hurtling, malefic rain. Heck gripped the rim of his helmet with his hands and pulled down hard but it was an impossible task to cover himself with it. Further explosions—a treetop crashed and Heck felt a rush of air as it landed heavily in the mud behind him. He tried without success to push himself forward into the rough wood. He desperately yearned for a muddy foxhole to crawl into. The overhead explosions were a continuous noise, too loud to be heard. Falling debris knocked occasionally against his helmet.

It all stopped suddenly. Only one voice was screaming now; the second had stopped. A few last dislodged branches rattled down. The screaming continued, but around that lone, terrible sound a perfect silence prevailed. A medic started toward the injured man. Heck, recalling his experience in Elbeuf, judged that an artillery pause could not be discerned from a stop and stayed in his place.

After a couple more minutes a sergeant came around reorganizing the unit. One man was dead, split open at the collarbone. Heck had to summon an effort of will to wrench himself away from the sight of split skin, glistening blood, exposed muscle, white bone. The other wounded man was sliced open on the leg, the back, and down the length of his arm. He was quiet now, glassy-eyed with morphine. The medic sprinkled packets of sulfa powder into the wounds. Two men were detailed to carry him back. Silently, at a signal from the sergeant, the remainder of the squad moved forward again, leaving behind the wounded and the dead.

The next night they moved again, sometimes in circling or contradictory directions, and initially Heck believed that they had become completely lost in the forest, that they might even have strayed behind the German lines. When the lieutenant had a map out he stood looking at it with his mouth ajar, an expression that did not convey confidence. Sometimes the non-coms could be heard arguing with him. But then they seemed to enter a relatively quiet area, and indeed they began to make movements by daylight, which made marching so much easier it was a tremendous relief, but at the same time all the light caused Heck to feel suicidally exposed. They marched along narrow trails and two-rut logging roads, through weed-filled firebreaks and across streams, uphill and down, past huts of unknown purpose, past isolated houses built of stone and built of wood, past piles of fallen trees and sections of burned forest, around shell craters and magnificently corroded, torn, broken, and scavenged jeeps, trucks, and antitank guns. The destroyed vehicles smelled of burned fuel and oil, scorched paint and steel and leather. The smell of the burned dead was like nothing else, and hours later when Heck's mouth grew dry he could taste it.

Deep into the pine forests there were peaceful places that possessed a cathedral's space and height and solemn stillness. Dropped limbs lay about like fallen statuary. Bird noises were rare and seemed to carry from far away. Moving through such a place they found an unexploded, finned bomb half-buried in the earth. An emaciated dog with long, matted fur, black around the face and white on the belly, sat atop the tube of the bomb and quietly regarded the soldiers as they passed. One of the men left behind an open C-ration can. They passed the isolated, upside-down turret of a tank whose lower parts were nowhere to be seen. Underfoot, roots showed out of the soft earth, twisted and vaguely obscene. Heck's feet swelled and blistered and he feared to take his boots off to look because he knew the boots would not go on again. Occasionally now the dog could be seen trailing along behind them. More food was left, and the men began to call her Pooch.

I've not been eating well, Heck thought. His perception of the world's nearer aspects was hazy. Often the rations he ate stayed down for only a few minutes before he vomited them out again. His stomach was painful with hunger and all he could do to try to pacify it was pour in a little water, and even the water, given a vile flavor by the army's purification tablets, made him queasy. Near the end of a day's march he could only think about the nearly impossible task of setting one foot before the other.

Then in the evening, near dark, they came into yet another position hidden among the trees, not far from a rutted two-track road. They had been moving for nearly twenty-four hours. Heck scratched a shallow hole for himself and lay in it. He was awoken abruptly by shouting and gunfire to his right. A couple of GIs ran frantically past him. A machine gun gnashed with terrible noise. The sergeant came to Heck's hole and shouted, "They're trying to flank us! Swing out that way!" Then he seized Heck under the shoulders and physically dragged him out.

Heck sat dumbly looking up at the sergeant. The sergeant ran off shouting, bullets churned the twilight gloom overhead, and finally fear sliced through befuddlement and Heck got up and ran in the direction that the sergeant had pointed. The machine gun stopped, but several rifles continued to peck away. A couple of men had run out in front of Heck, and Heck came up behind them and did as they did—ducked behind a tree and pointed his rifle in the direction of the excitement. The noise, however, had now dropped to the rhythm of a single rifle, steady as the blows of a lumberjack with an axe. One of the two men Heck had followed crept around his tree and moved forward. The other GI, a small, thick man, looked at Heck and Heck looked at him and they stayed where they were. Heck's breathing was ragged and loud and he could not control it. Despite the cold he sweated. He desperately feared something would emerge that he would have to shoot at. Then he desperately wished something would emerge that he could shoot at. The man creeping ahead had disappeared among the trees. The last rifle ceased firing, finally, and a brittle silence began. Heck sensed that whatever had happened was over, but his desire to shoot something remained. If he could just shoot something, then he could begin to feel like a soldier. He thought to himself—with such fierceness that he nearly said it aloud—*I am not a coward.* He aimed about twelve feet up into a nearby tree and crushed the trigger—but the trigger failed to move.

He had left the safety on. In disgust he slung the rifle on his shoulder and walked back to his foxhole.

The story that came around was that some Germans had been seen and shot at and they had run away. Two had been killed. Or maybe not, because no one could find the bodies. Conlee speculated that someone had begun shooting at shadows. Or they might have seen the advance group of a larger party.

But nothing more happened that night, and the next day they marched again.

Around midday they moved through a tiny deserted hamlet

of stone houses whose roofs had all been burned, exposing the buildings to the sky like open pustules. Obie was absurdly small and wiry under the weight of the radio he carried, but he never complained. He had established a reputation as a scavenger, and he often wandered away from the others to look into things. He found a sack of raisins in one of the buildings and he shared these around. Heck put them one at a time in his mouth and sucked on them like candies. They tasted of smoke and ashes but were nonetheless delicious.

Pooch came up and he offered her a few raisins, which she disdained. Heck felt conflicted toward her: he wanted to tell the bitch she could go, she should go. He reached down and rubbed her, whispering, "You idiot. You fool." She nosed at Heck's crotch and looked up at him with enormous brown and black eyes in an expression that might have been reproachful, then suddenly lost interest, turned and trotted ahead, past the men who called to her, and vanished up the road.

In a break in the pines, on a wide, muddy path they ascended a hill studded with oaks. Someone had cut an open space for a garden plot, filled with rows of dead plants. To one side lay a pile of abandoned German ammunition crates, blackening with mildew. A wooden toolshed not much larger than an outhouse stood in the back corner, leaning and sagging with age.

Ahead of Heck were Conlee and Obie. Obie was eating from his sack of raisins by the handful, and between mouthfuls of raisins he was saying to Conlee, "I'm glad I'm not fat."

Conlee did not reply. Ahead of Obie was a large man who carried a Browning automatic rifle—universally referred to as the BAR man—who commented, "You'd have lost the fat a long time ago."

"I think all this would be much more difficult, if I were fat," Obie said, then something cracked in the air and Obie stiffened as if to attention, his legs buckled, and the weight of his radio pulled him over.

Heck stared at the body, then looked around. Others with quicker instincts had already thrown themselves out of sight. A second shot snapped by. Heck scrambled off the trail, chased by a third and a fourth shot. He dropped into the mud of a shallow ditch, where he lay breathing heavily. Conlee crawled into the ditch beside him and whispered, "He's got to be in that shed we just passed." Heck peered around cautiously. A couple of the more veteran GIs were creeping away through the trees—they seemed to know what to do without consultation or orders. Conlee followed, and, more slowly, Heck moved after him.

Intent on keeping himself out of the line of sight of anyone in the shed, Heck lost track of the others. On his hands and knees he crawled ahead to one tree, then forward to another. There was a shot and Heck pressed himself flat. A loud furious volley followed. He thought, We've been ambushed. But the shooting ceased. Heck peered around his tree. He heard himself breathing as if he had been sprinting. He slowed his breaths and stood, pressing himself hard against the tree. A German had come out of the shed, holding his hands up. Conlee and several others appeared from various points, their weapons trained on the German. The shed was riddled with bullet holes. The German was bleeding from his shoulder. A GI strode up and put his M-1 into the German's back and prodded him toward the path.

The German moved stiffly, staring straight ahead. His lips moved—trembling, Heck thought at first, but then realized that the German was speaking silently and quickly to himself, praying perhaps. Heck glowered at him. He wanted to see the German weep or plead, cower or tear his hair out. The German did not, however, and none of the GIs emerging into the garden spoke. The only sounds were the scuffing of feet and the occasional gentle rattle of a metal buckle or button. The BAR man went into the toolshed and came out with the German's rifle and a couple of potato-masher grenades. The German reached the path, where he was allowed to stop. Conlee and a few of the other GIs gathered around him. The German gazed up into the branches of the trees, his lips moving rapidly. Heck stood among the others around the German. The BAR man wandered over, inspecting the mechanism of the German rifle. The German, gazing into the trees, intent on his whispers, seemed unaware of the Americans. Heck wanted to hit him. Suddenly, one of the GIs kicked the German in the back of the knees and he fell facedown on the ground, where, with his hands still extended up past his head, he moaned softly, then resumed whispering. Except for the BAR man, everyone had their M-1s trained on him. The German whispered. No one else spoke. There was a shot, a kernel of blood appeared on the German's back, and rapidly several more shots followed. The German shuddered slightly.

With a foot, someone rolled him onto his back. The front of his shirt was a mess of blood. His eyes gazed dully upward. His mouth gaped and his expression was as if he had eaten something disagreeable. Someone lit a cigarette. Someone muttered,

"Fucking bastard kraut." One by one the men began to move away.

Heck looked at Conlee, and Conlee said, "Don't look at me like that."

Heck didn't know where to move his eyes. They settled on gazing at the German again. He said, "He's dead."

Conlee knelt and probed the German's pockets. He pulled out a few folded papers, which he glanced through, then dropped. He said, "If the kraut had missed Obie, we would have sent him back as a prisoner. But he didn't miss and Obie is dead and now the fucking kraut is dead and that's justice as far as I see it." Conlee cleared his throat and spat on the corpse. "You see it different?"

The German's eyes were a shade of blue-green that reminded Heck of the sea and made him think of sitting on the cliff with Claire. Blood oozed from the German's chest and stomach. He looked to be about Heck's own age, and he might easily have come from some Iowa town, as Heck had, except for the uniform. Conlee's spit had landed on the dead man's neck and glistened there. Heck looked away and thought of how Obie had stiffened when he was shot. He said, "No."

But Conlee bore a look of philosophy now, as if he had forgotten Heck. He said, with great equanimity and something like longing, "Fuck." He shouldered his bag and set off after the others. Heck followed. The bodies were left where they lay for Graves Registration to find.

The BAR man carried the German sniper's rifle with him for several hundred yards along the trail, then, suddenly, he turned and with a howl and a step toward the trees he hurled the gun like a spear. Somewhere, invisibly, it rattled among the branches.

Heck found himself thinking of his father's pale hands and veined wrists, the reassuring clatter of his mother in the kitchen in the morning, her popovers, fresh from the oven, puncturing them with a fork and the steam releasing. He felt exhausted and ancient and absurdly young. He thought of how his father tended to look at him sidelong, rarely straight on, unless Heck was in trouble for something—an infrequent occurrence. He thought of Obie's family back home and felt bad for them. But after some miles his pity drifted toward the German. Obie had died without a moment to understand what had happened. But the German had understood that he was to die. Heck imagined the moment of fear before death to be worse than death itself. And the German, too, likely had a family that would mourn. Yet, simultaneously with these thoughts, Heck wondered if he should have fired his gun into the prisoner with the others.

He wanted out; he wanted to go back; he wanted to wake up.

That evening, as Heck was digging a new foxhole, a recent replacement, a dark-haired boy with freckles, pointed to a nearby log. He said, "Can I take that?"

"Sure," Heck said.

The boy with the freckles bent and seized the piece of wood, and Heck had a sudden, brief view of the complicated pattern of tree branches against the sky as an explosion threw him.

He next became aware of a loud monotone—his ears ringing. He pushed himself up. The world had an odd, washed-out appearance. The boy who had picked up the log had vanished. A hand lay off to one side. A boot stood nearby. No arm-torso-leg connected these. Heck looked at himself and saw that he was whole. The ground was covered with a thick spray of blood and gristle. One would not have thought a single man could be broken into so many parts. "Booby trap!" someone shouted, absurdly late. Heck lay back and stared upward, seeing nothing.

The next day it snowed for the first time. It came down in fat flakes that flickered against the darkness of the woods and sat in small white piles on the pine boughs. There was something terrible in seeing so familiar and beautiful a thing as snow in a place such as this—it fell in the same color and shapes of snow he had always known, it fell in the same swirling patterns from the same gray clouds, yet everything it fell on was different. In the snow the men plodded like refugees. It fell thick and slantingly, making the world a narrow white-and-gray blur and accumulated rapidly across the ground and atop helmets and weapons. Heck and the others scuffed at it, for in its insubstantiality and pervasiveness it seemed to represent the accumulation of their misery and troubles.

But in a clearing was Pooch, and she was overjoyed by the snow and ran to and fro, tossing it with her nose and jumping to snap at the drifting flakes. The helmeted head before Heck said, "Look at old Pooch. Look at her." And Heck, though he did not laugh, felt a little less unhappy.

That night the ground was already beginning to freeze and digging into it required an effort of chiseling and scraping with the blade of the entrenching tool. Heck's fingers were numbing, feet numbing.

Two days later, patches of skin on his hands had begun to blacken. He still did not dare look at his feet. He was filthy and unshaven and he felt a profound hunger beyond any he had known before. They had little proper cold-weather gear; they cut head and arm holes into their sleeping bags so that they could be worn and draped themselves in white sheets for the bare measure of camouflage the cloth provided against the white landscape. The removal of corpses from the snow left distinctive yellow stains. When Heck dreamed he dreamed of white and stains and his dreams were always nightmares.

At one time he had expected that the war would go by like a snake whose tail he would eventually see, and that would be the end. But now he saw it to be more like a river that is always going by and of which one expects no end. One day he watched a GI urinate into the open mouth of a German corpse. The next day he entered a town recently abandoned by the Germans and found the body of an American soldier who had been literally crucified.

One night the lieutenant broke up his pairing with Conlee, and Heck shared a foxhole with a new replacement, a broad-shouldered boy, a steelworker's son from Pennsylvania who seemed perfectly content with life in the war—he behaved like a union man nonchalantly going about his tasks among the blast furnaces. He claimed that the C- and K-rations tasted just fine, and when Heck had choked half of his down and prepared to toss the remainder away, the new kid took the stuff and ate it without hesitation. He did not complain about the mud; he did not complain about the cold. He told cheerful little stories about his childhood, about sledding into trees or playing football with a pumpkin or catching very large fish with his father. Then the sergeant came around and told them to be ready to move out at first light the next day, and when the sergeant had gone the new kid said, "Tomorrow, I'm not going. I'm done. I'm staying here. I like it here."

Heck looked around their hole in the frozen mud. He said, "You can't stay; they'll arrest you."

"Fine."

"Then you'll rejoin us?"

"No. I'm done."

"That's desertion."

"I'd rather call it being done."

"They'll shoot you."

"No, they won't."

"Deserters are shot."

"That's what they tell you, and theoretically they could. But you've got to look at it from a historical perspective."

"You don't think it will happen."

"I did my research, before shipping out. No one has been shot or otherwise executed for military desertion since the Civil War. No one. Eighty years. You think no one in the Africa or Italy campaigns deserted? You think not a single American in the entire First World War ever ran away? Of course they did. It happens all the time. The deserter might face court-martial and might be sentenced to be shot, but, historically, the sentence is always commuted. At worst, maybe they'll put me in prison. For how long? Maybe they'll keep me there for two or three years after the end of the war before they get tired of me and kick me out into the street."

"But they *could* shoot you."

"But they won't. This war will be over inside a year. Say I sit in jail for maybe another three years after that, I'll do four years' time altogether. That's a hell of a lot better than losing a leg or meeting a kraut bullet with my forehead, which are the only other ways I'm going to get out of this war. I mean, look around."

Heck felt unhappy and vaguely insulted. He said, with little conviction, "I should report you."

The Pennsylvanian laughed hard and said, "Please do. I would enjoy that, really I would. Please report me."

During the night Heck pondered this option, knowing he could not avail himself of it, uncertain why. He thought of his father in a more concrete way than he had in a long time. He tried to guess the temper of the silence his father would offer if Heck deserted. It was strange to think of his father, in Iowa, still putting together a newspaper every day, to think there were lives unchanged. He touched the silver of the music box.

The next day the Pennsylvanian was gone. The lieutenant asked Heck if he knew what had happened to the man, and Heck shook his head.

When the lieutenant was killed that evening—he was sitting on a tree stump somewhat in front of their position, waiting for an overdue patrol to come back, when a sniper shot him through the heart—everyone said it was a damned shame but why was he sitting out there anyway? There was dark comfort in the remembered foreknowledge that it had been bound to happen, sooner or later.

Unfortunately, positioned as the lieutenant was, no one dared go retrieve his body. The snipers were brutal, the body bait in a trap. So the lieutenant sat there, his hand raised to the top of his head as if rubbing his scalp thoughtfully. In the cold his face hardened with an expression of disdainful surprise, the look of someone attacked with a childish insult. From where

Heck peered out of his hole the lieutenant could be seen easily. It was a relief when, the following night, a strong wind came up and the body fell out of sight. A new lieutenant arrived, and word came around, in tones both ironic and incredulous, that the new man didn't appear nervous at all.

The new lieutenant ordered a nighttime "probe"—which meant, as Conlee explained it, wandering around until shot at, then running away. The noncoms argued against it, explaining that the snipers here had been particularly active. But the lieutenant would not back down. Such was the situation, anyway, that the sergeant described to Heck, Conlee, and Zeem as the four of them set out. They wandered around in the dark for several terrifying hours. Heck's hand strayed repeatedly to the silver music box in his pocket, always suspecting that this would be his last opportunity to touch it. Yet, incredibly, they encountered no one. As they were returning Conlee observed that their lack of casualties was beyond explanation. He seemed quite aggrieved at the lack of casualties.

They had spread out as they neared their holes in the first pallid light of day, and Heck had lost track of the others when he seemed to see a movement very near the company's position. He stood still a minute, but saw nothing more. He began to inch forward, thinking perhaps it had been nothing, or a movement of the wind, when he saw it again, low to the ground. With his battered heart whacking itself against his ribs, he checked the safety on his rifle and crept forward. It crossed his mind that if he could eliminate one of the snipers he would be something of a hero.

As he came closer he realized he was very close indeed to the position that they had been dug into for several days now—the movement he had seen was approximately where the dead lieutenant's body had been left.

Then he saw that it was the lieutenant himself moving, rolling slightly side to side and gently rattling the branches around him. Heck crept nearer. A figure was crouched awkwardly over the corpse. A German, Heck thought, looking for souvenirs or maps. After watching for a moment, with great slowness he crept ahead. He was surprised to note that he felt exhilaration. He wanted to kill this German.

But then he could see that it was nothing human at all, just some animal, seemingly headless. "Hey," he whispered. "Hey."

The thing backed up to extract itself—its head had been buried in the lieutenant's gut. It was Pooch. She saw Heck and wagged her tail. She nosed the corpse and looked up as if inviting him to join her. Her muzzle was matted and dark with blood. "Hey, Pooch," Heck said. "Whatcha doing, Pooch?" And the dog beat her tail about happily until he raised his rifle and fired.

The dog cowered low, tail tucked under her belly, whimpering. He had missed. He walked over and kicked the dog in the ribs. She ran off yowling.

He encountered Conlee peering around a tree with his rifle aimed from the hip. "I nearly killed you," Conlee said. "Was that you?"

"Pooch was eating the lieutenant."

"Shit."

"I just scared her."

"Fuck."

Heck went back to his foxhole. He had fired at the dog without thinking. It bothered him that he had missed.

6.

HECK COULD NOT HAVE SAID WITH CERTAINTY WHETHER IT WAS the next day, or the day after that, or perhaps it was the same day that they pulled out and began trekking again. Somewhere, where they stopped to rest and eat, he sat moving his hand vaguely before him, fascinated by it and the movement: it was as if he were able to perceive along some new dimension and he were grasping for something there. Then there was an odd sound, like a passing diesel truck with a badly tuned engine, but overhead. The sky was an unsettling origin for such a sound, and instinctively he cowered a little. He peered into the sky and spotted an odd, fat airplane with stubby wings. Zeem was seated nearby, and Heck asked him, "What is it?"

"Buzz bomb. V-1. Going to London." They watched it trundle across the sky. "Some fall short. Hear that noise cut out, get under cover. Things make a hell of a bang. Course sometimes they cut out then start up again. You never know." Zeem shrugged. Slouching in a posture of exhaustion, he rubbed his face and took off his helmet.

"Hey," said Heck. "What happened to your hair?"

Zeem felt at his head, then peered incredulously into the hollow of his helmet. He took out a fistful of loose hair. "Christ," he said. "Is this mine?" He pulled more hair from his helmet, gathering it into his hands as though he were cupping water. "Shit," he said. "Bald. I must look like you."

Actually it looked worse, because the hair had come free in random clumps from here and there on the head, creating a crude patchwork of exposed pink flesh.

"Think I can get sent home? Pick up a Purple Heart?"

At the next stop, or perhaps it was during the next march on the next day, Heck moved a little away from the others to relieve himself. He stood at the base of a thick pine, devoid of branches to twenty-five or thirty feet up, and his urine steamed against the wood. He swayed side to side a little, watching the sheets of vapor ripple upward, and as he buttoned up he continued swaying, like a tree in a light wind. He closed his eyes and lifted his arms slowly up and down, a sensation familiar from years before, when he was a child and would convince himself of the feeling of flying. He was flying. He remembered his father taking him up by the feet and whirling him around so that the blood went into his head until it seemed his face would burst. He raised and lowered his arms. The cold air moved through his coat and against his skin.

Abruptly he stopped and sat. He drew his legs up and pressed his face into his knees. He was going insane. The possibility was suddenly very clear to him. As was the temptation.

He recalled the German sniper's blue-green, empty eyes, the bold, dead stare, the incomprehension.

He felt possessed by a terrible fearfulness. He did not want to be dead or crazy or maimed. Yet these seemed his only options.

He must retain a hold on his mind. With that, perhaps, he could find a way to find Claire. When he thought of living, he thought of her. But first he must keep his sanity.

His habit of quiet had hardened. He knew now the sounds of a variety of shells, knew which were rising from behind him and which were falling toward him, knew how near they would strike and how big a bang they would make, knew that the one that would kill him would be the one he never heard. He knew that at any given moment there was a fair chance he could be dead in the next moment, and somehow he was not paralyzed by this knowledge.

He thought about Claire, fretted over her. He loved her for offering to him the feel of her skin, the smell of her, the sound of her incomprehensible words.

They bivouacked in the woods near a farm, and the cook made steaming potatoes and pork. It was the first hot food they had been offered since Heck had arrived. Conlee examined the meat on his plate and said this was ominous. Then he began to eat rapidly.

They were roused before dawn the next morning, told to prepare for an assault, and led along a downward, narrow road. They came to a place where the road turned and a short rocky cliff rose sharply along one side of the road and the earth dropped away rapidly on the other side. Shoved off the road and tumbled down into the woods below in terrible profusion were the dead, broken into pieces and rotting, emitting a smell thick and awful like a greasy haze. Nearly all of them were American infantry with the keystone badge of their own division, the 28th. Here lay a lower mandible, there a kneecap. The skin was going black. Heck and the others moved through quickly, because the scene was unendurable and because if the Graves Registration men had not come it must be dangerous.

Two Sherman tanks clanked behind them on the road. A lieutenant came out to meet the tanks and shouted, "We were supposed to get five!"

A noncom in the turret yelled back, "Well, you got two! One's back there stuck in the mud, one blew a track on a mine, and another slid sideways into a ditch trying to get around the one that hit the mine! So you got two!"

Heck's platoon worked slowly up a wooded hillside, through desultory artillery and sniper fire. They halted just short of open ground. Heck quickly carved a shallow hole in the earth and settled in. Before him, just beyond the trees, lay grass, a hill, houses upon it, a thin church spire. As Heck watched, artillery began pounding the houses. Plumes of smoke rose up. Holes appeared in roofs. A chimney collapsed. A brick house went down with a deep rumbling noise. The peaked wooden roof of the church steeple exploded. Smoke and dust merged into a seething black mass. From the village there came no response.

The pounding went on for perhaps an hour; then the artillery lifted, and sergeants began bellowing and hollering, and the assault began, everyone running, and after that it was all random chaos and shooting and explosions and people running, and shouting and screaming, dirt flying, Heck running, stumbling, running. He was scared and exhilarated and he felt like he must have misunderstood something or they had neglected to tell him something because he hardly understood where he was running to or what he would do there, but for now he was running and screaming and that was everything. Not until he needed to stop screaming and slow slightly to breathe did he realize he had run ahead of everyone—there was no one before him. He glanced back and saw a man vanish within an explosion. Heck stumbled, pelted by a scattering of fragments that might have been earthen or human. He regained balance and ran harder. Where was he going? Where? He ran. Ahead on the hill were damaged trees, pale rocks, the craters of shells, and all the buildings of the town. He could see the Germans—a fraction of a helmet here, a gun barrel there. Loud, just beside his ear, snapped the noise of a bullwhip cracking. A bullet, he thought. Then he glanced back, apprehending that the bullet might very well have come from behind him. He was shocked by his own speed; the others appeared hopelessly far behind. He saw a shallow crater ahead and leaped into it.

Orders had simply been to advance into the town—as if it were as simple as walking into a five-and-dime. Where should he go in the town? What should he do there? What about all those people who would be shooting at him? He had no answers. He had never received any training in how to assault a house, how to fight in a city.

To his left the twin Shermans were advancing, drawing torrential blazes of gunfire from half a dozen different buildings, the bullets rebounding off the steel armor with shrieks and zings and fluttering noises, and Heck was glad he was not nearby. In a laborious rhythm the tanks turned their long guns to destroy the occupants of one window frame after another. Heck saw, briefly, a German rise up on a roof and launch—with a roar of flame—a *Panzerfaust* rocket. An explosion engulfed a side of the nearest tank. Thick coils of black smoke streamed upward from around the turret. A hatch was thrown open. The men who scrambled out were shot down one by one.

It now seemed impossible that he would ever raise himself up and move forward again. Death would be certain. Yet Heck felt relatively calm. He had reached this place safely, and he might not be able to escape it without dying, but at the moment, in this hole, he felt secure. He was able to look around himself with a kind of rational curiosity. The others behind him were cowering like himself. Only occasionally somewhere on the hillside did a GI appear out of his hiding place and dart into a new hole. Mortar and artillery shells shrieked and exploded. One by one these nudged Heck back toward fear.

Perhaps this same thought was occurring to others as well because suddenly several emerged and there was a flurry of motion and activity. A lieutenant stood full upright with his back to the Germans and howled insults at the men below him. The German machine guns renewed their furious chains of noise. Men began moving uphill.

Heck turned forward. He hesitated and shut his eyes. He heard the noises of hell erupting, screams like laughter, screams like a language. The smells of earth and burning and blood and cordite, of dust, smoke, and fear. The crack of a bullet passing. The thud of another burying itself in the dirt. He opened his eyes and saw the enemy guns ahead spitting small flames. His legs and hands trembled remarkably. He noticed a harsh rasp in his throat and wondered if he had been screaming. He felt the fear again, the surfeit of dreadful emotion that had paralyzed him in Elbeuf, the horrible sensation of losing control of himself, or of there being no control to have. Then a nearby blast lifted him slightly and dropped him—filling his mouth with dirt, which he nearly inhaled, causing him to gag and spit and spit, breaking the paralysis. He looked up and there were GIs around him, a few ahead of him. A blast pushed his helmet down against his head. He felt the shells were narrowing on him, and he scrambled out of his hollow and into the open. He got to his feet and lurched ahead. He ran.

A man in front of him spun violently and dropped—he lay with his arm taken off and several ribs exposed. Heck stepped over the detached arm and kept going. He was feeling, however, an accumulation—as if he were becoming heavier with each step, the fear returning into him like a tide. Yet he was nearly to the top of the hill, where there was a low stone wall he could hide behind. An explosion to his right lurched him sideways and down to his hands and knees. It seemed like an insult and he felt bitterly abused. He regained his feet and in a great struggle wrestled one foot uphill, then the other, watching the wall, nearing, until with enormous relief he pressed himself against its rough, cold stones.

He looked back at the other men coming up the face of the hill, to his left, to his right, and was shocked to see how effortlessly and rapidly they moved. They stared grimly ahead and ran headlong. The explosions that had seemed to be everywhere around Heck a moment before were actually quite scattered and appeared almost harmless from this perspective. The men moved with great agility and although he had reached this point ahead of them, Heck could not reconcile himself to the idea that he had himself come up the hill with equal or greater speed.

The wall he hid behind extended only, at most, thirty feet in either direction, and most of the men continued past it, directly into the streets and buildings, out of sight. The surviving Sherman tank propelled itself up the main road and disappeared in the village, hurling loud destruction ahead of itself.

Four other men had joined Heck behind his wall. One of them, a tall man with a fleshy, pink face, was lugging the weight of a Browning automatic rifle while another, smaller man was preoccupied with carrying ammunition for the BAR. With calm, quick efficiency, as if engaged in a fairly uninteresting field exercise, the BAR man and his ammo carrier set up and checked the weapon, then pushed it over the wall and began issuing short bursts of fire, moving from left to right, then back again. The BAR man took his hand off the gun and waved forward. "Go! Go! It's clear! Fucking go!" Heck exchanged glances with the other men. One stood and put a foot on the wall and leaped over. The man to Heck's left followed and quickly Heck—anticipating the exploding pain of a bullet in his chest but at the same time experiencing something like joy—went after him.

His foot caught somehow in the stones of the wall and he fell face-first on the other side. He put a hand out to somewhat arrest his fall, but the butt of his M-1 was driven into his chest, forcing the air from his lungs. He lay gasping while sudden white shapes faded slowly from his vision. Mentally he cursed himself. It seemed he was doomed to spend the entire war falling on his face. The BAR man and his ammo carrier clambered over the wall and the BAR man looked down at him. "You all right?" Heck nodded and waved them on. He made a show of pushing himself up, and the other two ran off.

He was alone in a space of high grasses and weeds. In front of him was a row of fruit trees and a two-story house. The BAR man and the ammo carrier kicked in the front door and rushed inside. There were shots. In the background hovered a tumult of explosions, machine guns, screams.

Heck circled around, along the wall. Where the wall ran beside the street it became higher—seven or eight feet tall. Patches of dead ivy fluttered dryly upon it. He reached an arched gateway, peered out, then stepped through.

In the street lay a dead cow. Directly across from him stood an intact, two-story half-timbered house, painted pale blue between the dark timbers. Farther down, several houses were burning, throwing billows of smoke upward as if intent on filling the sky. There were a couple of bodies, and a GI was sprinkling sulfa power into the empty socket of his own eye. The fighting seemed to have already swept onward, but Heck remained cautiously crouched beside the gate a minute. Then he began to creep along the street. Without ever entirely losing his fear, his awareness of death's proximity, he felt also a giddiness of triumph. He felt part of a tremendous victory. He ran farther down the street. Splashes of blood lay upon the cobblestones. A cat hissed at him. In a side yard was a corporal who was single-mindedly shooting open cans. He saw Heck and waved one of the cans, shouting, "Caviar!"

He had advanced past four houses altogether when a sudden series of shots startled him and he ducked behind the corner of a fence and waited. Initially it seemed the shots came from nearby, at him, but then he wasn't sure. He felt disinclined to expose himself to further dangers. He had exhibited great bravery already today—he thought, with a notion of indignation—in leading the charge up the hill. He decided he would turn back and reconnoiter down the opposite side of the street. He sprinted across the street and moved carefully from one point of cover to the next, glancing in doorways but not entering. A jeep careened by with an officer who shouted at him incomprehensibly.

He came to the pale blue, half-timbered house opposite the fenced yard and gateway through which he had entered the street. Squatting here at the corner of the house was a GI, tall and fair-haired. He was smoking a cigarette. Approaching him, Heck had the disconcerting impression that the other man had been watching him awhile. As Heck came up the other GI said, indicating the house at his back, "You know if anyone cleared this one yet?"

"No, I don't know."

The GI had thick ugly swaths of acne across his cheeks and forehead. He nodded and stubbed out his cigarette. "Suppose it might as well be me and you." He pushed himself out of his squat and moved toward the doorway. He stopped and pressed his back against the wall beside the doorway, took a grenade from his pocket, yanked the pin, held the grenade a moment longer, then tossed it in the open doorway. As soon as it exploded he swiveled and fired inside. He stepped forward, and Heck lost sight of him in the inner darkness and the smoke curling out. He could hear the sporadic shots. He edged forward. The other soldier shouted something—"C'mon," it might have been. Heck bent low and ran through the doorway.

He entered a foyer. The grenade had created a ragged, smoking hole in the floor and a wall. Fragments of wood, glass, and dried flowers had been thrown about. There were two doorways and a wide set of wooden stairs going upward. Heck looked at the dried flowers scattered at his feet. There was a gunshot upstairs. Heck crept to the stairs, watching the top. He noted with surprise how little fear he felt.

He climbed upward. At the top was a short hallway sprinkled with plaster dust and shards of paint that had come off the walls and ceiling. Smoke grayed the air. There were three doors, all open, and he could see the blond GI moving about in the nearest room. Heck glanced into the other two rooms, both of which contained mattresses, dressers, lamps, and other furniture in varying states of ruin, then joined the other GI.

This had evidently been a study—there was a large desk, and ranks of empty bookshelves covered one wall. Opposite hung a crossed pair of swords. Above was a gilt-framed photo of Hitler and on either side dangled red, white, and black pennants. A jumbled pile of paper and books lay on the floor and the blond GI was prodding through these with the muzzle of his rifle.

"Was there anyone up here?" Heck asked.

"Nope."

Heck crossed the room to a tall window beside the bookshelves and, standing cautiously at one side, peered out. From here he could see across much of the town. An explosion boomed and flickered down the street. Streams of smoke rose from burning houses. A downcast prisoner was ushered along with a rifle in his back. A pair of GIs ran by with their arms full of Nazi paraphernalia—flags, medals, swords, caps, armbands—and not far away was a soldier who appeared to be cooking steaks over a bonfire of velvet upholstered chairs. The food seemed such a wonderful thing that Heck was tempted to go down to join him.

The blond GI came up beside him. "Krauts didn't put up much of an argument over this place."

Heck glanced at him, and saw that the other man was offering him a bottle. Heck took it. He searched the label and found the word *Cognac*. After drinking a little he handed it back. "Where did you find that?"

"What I'm afraid of is that they're planning to come back." The blond GI took a slug of the liquor, then dropped it into his gas-mask pouch, which was otherwise empty. Heck wandered over to the desk. In one corner lay a round, egg-shaped hand grenade that appeared to be from the previous world war, and a black lacquered box ornamented with silver eagles and swastikas and several framed photos. Moving closer, Heck saw that the photos were of smiling men in black SS uniforms. There was a strange incongruity between their amiable, smiling faces and the coal-black uniforms. The paint on the grenade was peeling, and around the top were patches of rust. The lacquered box might have contained writing instruments or knives or possibly currency. Heck reached to feel the glossy surface.

"Hey," the tall GI said. "Tsk, tsk. Don't put anything past the krauts. They're sour-hearted fuckers."

Heck recoiled from the box, suddenly sick with the memory of the log that had exploded, the boy broken from his hand, his foot. He stepped into the hall, and the tall GI joined him, pointed his rifle back through the doorway, and blasted the desktop with a series of shots. "Nope," he said cheerfully. "It's okay."

Heck followed him back inside. The other GI strode over to the desk, where the lacquered Nazi box had been punctured with three or four splintered holes and knocked back against the wall. Fragments of the framed photos of happy SS men were scattered across the desk and floor. The grenade had fallen to the floor. The tall GI undid the clasp on the front of the lacquered box and swung it open and Heck was hurled backward into the hallway by the explosion. On his back on the floor, he had a brief moment of extreme lucidity during which he seemed able to see in all directions simultaneously: the fragments of flesh thrown against the wall behind him, the empty helmet at his feet, the smoke swirling in the doorway, the upset flies slowly coming to rest again on the ceiling, and even from above, down at himself, dotted with blood that might have been his own or the other man's, his eyelids sinking.

There followed an all-encompassing, black incomprehension.

What he knew next was the heaving of his chest, the moisture of tears or sweat or blood on his face. Somehow, he was on his feet. Somehow, he had come downstairs. He pressed his hands and face against a wall; he could not remember how he had gotten down here. He stepped back and wiped at his face. On his hands was blood. All the front of his torso felt bruised. He found his rifle lying in the corner. In his mind he had an image of the tall GI, exploding apart, hurtling toward him.

From the street came a strange, high, howling noise, like the screaming of an animal. Heck felt himself over and could identify no wounds. He could not entirely believe this and checked again. He could find no injury and felt no pain, only a terrible exhaustion. The animal howling continued in the street and Heck crept to the door and peered outside. An American soldier was seated on the curb with his feet in the gutter, head in his hands, gasping and wailing. His rifle and helmet were neatly arranged on the street before him. There were noises of nearby fighting. Heck suddenly wanted very badly to be out of this house. He gathered himself for a moment, then, gripping his rifle, darted past the GI on the curb and across the street toward the protection of the stone wall. He heard a pair of shots. His balance was shaky; he felt as if he were on the deck of a ship pitching in high seas.

He entered through the gateway and threw himself down beside the wall. His chest throbbed painfully. He twisted and saw the wailing man now sprawled on his back, silent.

He crawled along the wall into what would have been the back lawn. He reached a corner where the wall turned ninety degrees, and there he rested a minute, then put his helmet on the end of his rifle and raised it up over the top of the wall. It provoked no response. The fighting sounded not far away, and he could imagine that everyone was preoccupied with others than himself. In a quick slithering movement, he went over the wall.

He crouched on the other side a moment. Nothing happened. On this side of the wall he was hidden in a thick growth of brush and trees. There was a woman on the ground, half-hidden in the brush. Her eyes were closed. Her shoulder was a mess of blood. One breast was exposed, and nearly blue. She was dead; Heck recognized this calmly. His own calm was strange to him. He wondered, How had she come to be here? She was dressed in a long, soiled skirt and appeared young, but gaunt, with lines at the corners of her eyes. Perhaps she had for some reason failed to flee the town with the other civilians and had been caught out here by the shelling. Perhaps she had been a soldier's lover. Heck thought, hopelessly, of Claire. Grimly, trying not to touch the body, he stepped over her. With an awkward gait, bent low, he moved along the wall, passing along the back side of the house, until he came to the point where the brush gave out. Here he edged forward on hands and knees.

He was upon the hill he had charged to reach the town. The distance he had crossed in that charge now looked rather small. The earth was torn and shredded everywhere, and the dead and wounded lay scattered about, with several medics moving among them.

He crept back into the brush and peered over the wall. Thick black smoke streamed from a pair of upper-story windows in the house that the BAR man and his ammo carrier had charged into. Heck hunkered down with his back to the wall. He fretted briefly over whether he should go back into the town and rejoin the fighting. His orders, however, had been to get into the town, and he had done that. He was too tired to fight effectively. He would rest here a little and rejoin the others soon, if they hadn't finished the job yet.

Even among the not-distant noises of explosions, shots, screams, the crash of a building in collapse, he slept.

The death of the tall soldier, however, was not easily forgotten, and at the sound of an explosion Heck seemed to see again the tall GI hurled toward him, in fragments, and he woke with a start.

He wiped at his arms and the front of his shirt. The craggy bushes before him were peaceful and beautiful. The sounds of battle continued behind him; the fighting had perhaps grown nearer. He understood, slowly, that he had been asleep only a few minutes. He twisted and peered over the wall again.

Flames, pale in the sunlight, were tonguing out of the upper-story windows, and thick smoke now came from the ground-floor orifices. A section of the roof collapsed and flames and sparks shot high. He felt the heat on his face.

He thought then of Claire, how he wanted badly to return and find her and help her. He wanted to do this with a severity that ached in him.

Dimly, through the smoke and the gateway in the wall, he saw a figure run by in the street; then another went by, then a third. They were running out of town. The sounds of shooting had distinctly moved closer. He saw a couple more figures scurry by. They seemed to be American.

Heck sat down again behind the wall. They might have been wounded, evacuating themselves, or messengers of some kind, perhaps, or a tank crew that had lost their vehicle. He turned and peered over once more. If they were in retreat, he could not stay here.

The heat from the burning house was growing intense. The paint was cracking and blackening. Flames shot from every window. The smoke was now too thick to be seen through. With wobbling reluctance, Heck moved farther along the wall, out of the brush and toward the hillside he had charged up.

He reached a corner where the wall turned. He peered cautiously around, then followed the turn.

He stopped to rest. For a minute he sat without thinking. He felt in his pockets for a D-bar or something to eat. A sudden, rapid series of crashes and flakes of stone flying caused Heck to drop facedown. A machine gun, he thought, a machine gun had opened up on him. Perhaps he had allowed his helmet to rise a couple of inches above the wall. The gun pounded a few more shots into the stone wall at his back, silenced, then chattered in another direction. Heck felt at his face and helmet, scarcely believing that his head had not been split open.

Looking down past the length of the wall he could see a man here, a man there, darting out of the village and across the open ground. The clamor of fighting continued inside the town, but it had grown very close again. It seemed the Americans were being thrown out.

Heck felt despair, and for a moment he envied the dead their invincibility. He huddled, seeking to reduce his size as a target to nothing. It was impossible not to feel ungainly and huge. The machine gun hammered a few more shots into the wall. It was difficult to imagine how the Germans had already moved a machine gun into a position so near, and it seemed the Germans must be soldiers of incredible qualities. Occasionally bullets snapped overhead. He was, for the moment, behind the wall, secure. The zone of danger was there above him. It was as if there was a plane above which exposed flesh would be destroyed. Like sticking your hand into a threshing machine.

Suddenly a vast temptation opened—as though, not realizing he was near the sea, he had climbed a small berm, and there lay an ocean before him. He could extract himself from this deathfield; he could go back to Claire; all he had to do was put a hand up high enough to get shot. It would be far better than shooting himself in the foot: an enemy bullet, he didn't have to pull the trigger, and who could doubt him, shot in battle by an enemy machine gun. He needed to do it to retain his sanity, to escape death, to try to return to Claire. Right hand or left? He held the stock of his M-1 in his right hand and examined the left, the dirt-filled lines of the palm, the knuckles, the nicotine stains, the ragged nails. It was filthy and abused but nonetheless a thing whole and complete. He could feel the chill of the air against it. Stretching the fingers he felt the tendons pulling, the skin going taut. With little fear and more resignation he raised it up over the wall into the line of fire. The German machine gun was still gnashing and sending bullets whistling overhead, seemingly filling all the air with potential injury. Yet he held his hand up there, fingers outstretched, and nothing happened. The machine gun rattled mechanically, the bullets snapped by, and his hand was just there. He began to feel impatient and he pushed his hand up higher. A bullet passed so near his fingers he felt the disturbance of the air. Then the firing shifted toward another direction. He wagged his fingers a little. His shoulder began to grow tired. He felt awesomely frustrated.

Then, simultaneous with the sound of a single shot, his arm was hit with a hammer, knocking it backward with great violence, straining his shoulder and creating an explosion of pain that subsided so quickly he wondered if he had imagined it. No, he could still feel a pulsing of heat. His hand seemed to return to him slowly and mechanically, like flag being run down a pole. He could contract and move his fingers still; he could feel them. An intense movement of sparks passed through his hand and all along his arm, and when he thought at last to look at his hand, to *look* at it, it was with the eerie feeling of recalling a form of perception he had momentarily forgotten.

He sat looking at his hand and doubting himself, because there appeared to be nothing wrong with it. The fingers were all there, the thumb, the skin lay intact and taut across the palm. Turning the hand over, however, he noticed a small hole in the sleeve of his coat, then another on the opposite side, and the blood seeping into the cloth. He pushed up the sleeve of his coat and his shirt and here was the wound, neatly through the wrist, bleeding freely on either side. The fingers of his hand trembled violently, but it hardly hurt. He could still move his fingers, although when he did blood spurted weakly. There was a heat in his hand. He needed to find a medic.

When he looked up he saw Conlee watching from the other end of the wall. It was the first familiar face Heck had seen since they'd begun the charge up the hill, and for a second he and Conlee stared at each other; then Conlee smiled and moved toward him in a rapid squat-crawl. "Looks like you got yourself a boo-boo there. Better go back and get patched up." The machine-gun fire stopped, and Conlee raised up to fire a few shots over the wall, then flung himself down as the German gun resumed its efforts. Conlee grinned. "Terrible, something like that happens, bullet catches you like that. Really unfortunate." He locked eyes with Heck and grinned. Then he turned and crawled away.

It entered Heck's mind—without any particular hope for or against the possibility—that Conlee might be killed. He noted that he himself might be the one to do the killing, but he had no desire for it; he would rather accept the consequences of what he had done. He felt too tired to do anything but accept. His arm began to throb with pain. He peered over his shoulder, looking for a secure route rearward.

7.

THE SNOW-FILLED FIELDS SHONE WHITE AND SMOOTH IN THE sun. Smoke from a farmhouse chimney carried a warm, familiar scent of burning pine. Behind the farmhouse stood a square wooden barn with ranks of glittering icicles long as rifles hanging from the roof's edge, the teeth of a beautiful monster.

At the door to the house a GI shuffled his feet and smoked a cigarette. His rifle was propped casually against the wall. Heck explained who he was, offered his papers. The sentry nodded and opened the door.

Inside Heck could see nothing; the windows were blacked out and the house seemed dark as night after the glare of the sun on snow. He stood blinking. Gradually he began to be able to see figures seated around a large, cast-iron stove in the corner. All the chairs in the room—plush armchairs, wooden dining chairs, a bench—had been pulled over to that source of warmth. Socks, pants, underwear, and coats hung on ropes above the stove. Heck peered at the soldiers seated below.

After he had taken the wound to the wrist, Heck had made his way to the nearest medical station. They were unimpressed with his injury, and he was billeted in a nearby barn to rest until the hole in his wrist sealed up. The division couldn't afford to lose men to superficial wounds, and Heck had no will to argue about it.

A couple of days later, however, his division, the 28th, had been taken out of the Hürtgen and sent to a quiet part of the line to rest and cycle in replacements. The medical station followed the division, and Heck was put into another cot in another barn.

Early one morning noises of heavy artillery and fighting erupted in the distance and over the next hour began to move nearer. Soldiers in a jeep came through shouting crazy things. Soon there were scores of people in full retreat—not an organized, military retreat but a panicked, everyone-for-himself retreat that became a flood, moblike; men who had abandoned their equipment, vehicles, artillery, rifles, and ammunition fled past the medical station without looking anyone in the eye. It was the beginning of the fighting that became known as the Battle of the Bugle. Heck and the other ambulatory wounded were sent out to fend for themselves, and Heck wandered westward alone for a couple of days. He ended up at a depot where he spent several weeks, loading and unloading trucks. By the time order was restored and Heck was sent to rejoin his proper unit, it was near the end of January 1945.

In the farmhouse, one of the figures detached from the

group at the stove and came toward Heck. Although Heck could see only dimly, he knew by the silhouette's shape and movement that it was Conlee. "Hello, Heck," Conlee said.

He sounded friendly enough, although he didn't offer to shake hands. Heck's hands were occupied with his rifle and his pack anyway. Heck hesitated, then said, "Hello, Conlee." It was unsettling how old Conlee looked. Heck knew the man was only eighteen, but anyone would have guessed at least thirty. After a moment of nervous silence, Heck offered, hesitantly, "I'm glad you're all right."

"I'm doing okay. I don't know if you'll recognize much of anyone else. You might as well go take a place over by the stove and warm up. I'll introduce you to all the new ones."

Heck was not sure how to take this friendliness. He looked at the stove. "Is Zeem here?"

Conlee frowned and straightened slightly. "Zeem stepped on a mine. Looked like he might be able to keep one leg, one testicle."

"Oh, God." Heck set his bag down and rubbed his face.

Conlee said, "Go on, warm up."

Heck picked up his bag again. Moving past Conlee, he noticed stripes and stopped. "Sergeant?"

"Yeah. Don't congratulate me, please. It's just a matter of somehow still being alive and in one piece. Go on. I'll be there in a moment."

Heck failed to absorb the names offered to him around the stove. A couple of the faces he recognized as boys who had been fresh replacements at the time he was shot. The others had come in sometime afterward, although to look at the lines around their eyes one would have thought they had been in combat for years.

He gathered from the conversation that they would remain here several days longer, perhaps as much as a week, while more replacements were integrated and the generals decided where they wanted to move this particular chess piece. Their current location was considered very lucky, and something of a coup. A house! With a stove! The boys hadn't yet gotten over it. Before, to stay in a barn was a luxury. But here the barn was used only for a kitchen, and the men trooped out three times a day for hot meals. Three hot meals!

Just past the iron stove was a room that the platoon's lieutenant had made into an office, with a couple of chairs and a large oak table that had been taken from the kitchen and was now strewn with papers. Conlee wandered in and out freely, and at times when the lieutenant was off somewhere, it unofficially became Conlee's office. He said nothing about the matter of Heck's wound. In fact, after the first conversation at the door he seemed to pay no particular attention to Heck, and Heck was uncertain what this meant. Perhaps Conlee had decided to forget it, to offer Heck another chance. Perhaps he was waiting to bring it up at the most embarrassing possible moment. Perhaps he was biding time until a convenient opportunity to put a bullet in Heck's back.

The others understood Heck to be a veteran, nearly as veteran as Conlee himself, and they deferred to his silence. He had been wounded by an enemy bullet and it hadn't gotten him out of the war—this could only be very bad luck indeed, so they perhaps thought it understandable that he would hold himself apart a little and brood on his lot. Heck felt as if he ought to disabuse them—make a suggestion to the effect that he was nothing but a coward. But anything short of an outright confession would be interpreted as modesty, and he could not imagine trying to explain what he had done in believable detail.

During the next three days the sky had an extraordinary clarity, a blue that receded behind itself indefinitely. A wind gusted erratically off the fields, lifting and dissipating high shimmering plumes of snow. There was one salient event during this time. Heck and the others were lined up at the door of the barn for lunch, standing with arms crossed, stamping their feet, breathing small whorls of condensation into the wind and muttering in anticipation of hot stew, bread, and coffee. One by one they were served by the cook, and Heck was nearly to the doorway when there was a sudden, loud crack.

Inside Heck's mind, the report was immediately followed by an anticipation of his own death. But it was the man before him who collapsed, screaming as he fell, his shriek broken by a gurgle, which had also ceased by the time Heck had dropped flat beside him. Others did likewise, or scattered into the barn or toward the house, where nearly everyone had left their weapons. "Where's the sniper?" screamed one GI, his voice high-pitched with panic. "Where's the fucking sniper?" Heck lifted his face off the ground and saw directly before him the oozing wound in the man's shoulder. A thing jutted from the wound, oddly shaped, shining—metallic he thought, adrenal fear still frantic inside him. But it was transparent. It was ice.

Conlee crouched beside him. "Icicle," he said. "A fucking icicle." He checked for a pulse. Heck sat up. There was a gap in the rank of icicles suspended from the barn's roof. A medic came.

Conlee stood and bellowed, "Calm down! There's no kraut sniper." He glanced at the roof. "Better move away from there," he said to Heck and the medic.

The medic drew out the icicle, a lance of ice nearly four feet long. The tapering end had noticeably thinned in the body's heat and glowed pink.

The remaining icicles over the barn door were knocked down with noisy shots from a Browning. They lay in small heaps of dazzling shards. Lunch was eaten quietly. Someone mentioned that the dead man had survived a month of combat, including the attack that became the Battle of the Bulge.

It could have happened outside a barn in Iowa, but it had happened here, and Heck turned the event around and around in his mind until he could see nothing in it but the tapering pink end of the icicle.

On the afternoon of his third day at the farmhouse a GI tapped him on the shoulder and pointed at the office. "Conlee wants to see you."

From behind the desk Conlee asked Heck to shut the door, then offered a cigarette. They sat smoking. Conlee gazed at the window. Blackout curtains had been pushed aside, and the window framed a tree: snow sat in crooked white lines atop the crooked black lines of its branches.

Conlee said, his tone conversational, "We held that town, you know. A lot of men died holding on to that town." Then, stubbing out his cigarette, Conlee added, "You were cited as an expert marksman during your training."

"What?"

"Expert marksman. Is that right?"

Heck looked out the window, past the tree toward the barn

denuded of icicles, then glanced at Conlee again. Basic training had been something that had happened a thousand years ago. Conlee bore an expression of mild expectation. Heck said, tentatively, "Yes."

Conlee gestured at some of the papers. "The lieutenant has been asked to provide an expert marksman for a special assignment. I suggested your name. Is that all right?"

With the door closed, the heat from the stove in the other room was not getting in, and Heck could feel the cold gathering. He waited, but Conlee offered no more. "Yes," Heck said. "Okay."

"There's no danger involved. Don't worry. A truck will be here at 0600 tomorrow. Take your M-1. You'll be in a little town in the Vosges Mountains." Conlee shifted some papers and pointed to a dot on a map. "Sainte-Marie-aux-Mines—" Conlee pronounced the name slowly, Americanizing the French: *Saint Mary ah Mines.* "You'll be there for a couple of days, then you'll rejoin us." Conlee gazed at him for a moment, then turned away and picked up some papers and began to shuffle them.

Heck went to the door, but hesitated. "Can't you tell me what this is?"

"You'll be given further orders there."

"All right."

At the fire, someone else had taken his seat. Heck settled into another, farther from the warmth. He wondered if it was possible that Conlee was actually trying to give him some kind of lucky break. He closed his eyes and leaned back in his chair and tried not to wonder, tried not to dread. But still the image in his mind was of a pink, narrowed icicle.

When Heck boarded the deuce-and-a-half—it arrived half an hour late—he counted nine other GIs already on board. All wore the red keystone patch of the 28th Division, but they were from other units within the division and Heck did not know any of them. By the stiffness and distance of how they sat relative to one another he sensed that no one knew any of the others. The truck made two more stops. Then, with a dozen men on board, it headed south as fast as the roads would allow. The men smoked, and occasionally someone would say a few words to the person next to him, about the roads, which were surprisingly smooth, or the weather, which was gray and misty. They spoke in near whispers, however, and the talk never sustained itself past a few terse exchanges. Heck pondered the mystery of their task with alternating alarm and weariness. He suspected that the others knew more than he did and what they knew was bad, or there would be chatter, questions, speculation.

Beside him sat a freckled young man who kept a wad of tobacco in his mouth and spit from time to time onto the floor of the truck. Occasionally, as if insulted by some inner voice, the freckled man scowled. After the truck had stopped for fuel and a short rest, Heck said to him in a low voice, "What is it we're supposed to do? Do you know?"

The freckled man's face swiveled to stare at him. The tobacco was a lump in his cheek, and his tense expression shifted slightly toward incredulity. "What do you mean?"

"What is it we've been volunteered for? Do you know?"

"You don't know?"

"They didn't tell me anything."

The freckled man shook his head, then leaned forward, put

his elbows on his knees and spit on the floor. A minute passed, and Heck realized there would be no answer. He pulled his head down into the collar of his coat.

Nearing the last hour of daylight, they began to pass on their right humpbacked hills veiled in gray mists. Slowly these resolved into forested slopes, hundreds of feet high, a square castle tower at the top of one, the snow-white slopes marked with the black strokes of innumerable trees. The truck turned into a valley, and the trees spread down off the hills to meet the sides of the road. It was a tremendously beautiful landscape. They passed through a small town, then another, nestled into the crook of the valley. There were gabled buildings painted pink, brown, rust, or lavender, with dark wooden window shutters.

Then a sign said *Sainte-Marie-aux-Mines*. At the heart of town were two- and three-story buildings set jowl to jowl, some with signs: *Boulangerie* or *Boucherie*. The church tower had a pointed steeple atop a rounded dome, like the spiked helmets of the kaiser's army in the previous war. They stopped outside a square, gated, institutional-looking building with an American flag over the doorway.

They unloaded and walked through the gates and up the short path to the door. The freckled man beside Heck said, without looking at him, "They should have told you. We're here to shoot a deserter. We're the firing squad."

"What?" Heck said.

The freckled man strode ahead. Heck understood what had been said, but understanding seemed to leave him uncomprehending again, in a cycle, fast and flickering, white and dark.

A voice behind Heck said, "Something wrong?" and Heck

realized he had stopped. He was blocking the doorway. The freckled man disappeared down a hallway, and Heck stumbled after him.

They were billeted in two ranks of bunks in a large room. On the wall beside Heck's bunk was a blackboard, and a crowd of school desks stood in a corner—they were in a schoolhouse. Still hardly anyone spoke. The men wrote letters, smoked cigarettes. Heck's thoughts tried and failed several times to achieve some order. He thought to himself, "I do not understand." But he did. It seemed he should have questions, but he could not think of what the questions should be. He wanted to break something, but the things to be broken were impossible to break, and he sat not moving.

Presently a lieutenant walked into the room and Heck stood, operating under trained habit. The lieutenant said, "At ease." He looked several years older than Heck, with broad shoulders and a narrow waist, and he appeared untroubled, calm. Heck could nearly convince himself that the freckled man had been lying, making an awful joke perhaps, and now the truth would emerge.

But the lieutenant, though he seemed calm, held his silence ten seconds, then longer, while everyone stood looking at him, and the dilating silence broke Heck's hope.

The lieutenant said, "As you know, we are here to execute a man, a Private Slovik, for the crime of desertion. I don't suppose it's a task any of us likes. But you shouldn't feel bad about it." The lieutenant moved his gaze from face to face. "The man deserted. Twice, in fact. He was tried in a fair court. We are here simply to implement a decision made by those authorized to do so. There is no need for you to feel bad or upset about your task.

The man is a condemned coward, who willfully and knowingly abandoned his unit. All we are here to do is carry out a sentence."

The lieutenant continued talking a while longer, but to Heck it seemed the man was only repeating himself in synonymous phrases, possibly trying to convince himself as much as the others. He hated the lieutenant for his face of calm.

The lieutenant ended by saying, "We will go through the whole procedure tomorrow, so you'll know exactly how it goes. The execution itself will take place the following morning. Are there any questions?"

Heck thought to himself, *Will take place.*

There were no questions asked. The lieutenant departed, and a minute later a corporal came in and led them to another room for supper.

The food was good—mutton stew and dense bread and a vinegar-doused potato salad and little berry pies. Heck ate meagerly and without hunger. The other men began to talk in low voices. The windows were painted black. Pages tacked to the wall offered French words in the ungainly script of children's handwriting. Beside Heck was a big-gutted, pink-cheeked man, soon advancing into his second helping of stew, who said to the GI across from him, "I asked if there wasn't a way I could get out of this. Asked the captain. Captain said, 'Not unless you want to take his place.' " With his stew spoon in midair the pink-cheeked man brayed in a mirthless imitation of laughter. "Some choice."

Heck asked him, "What's the name again? The man we're—?"

"Slovik."

That night Heck lay gripping the silver music box with both hands on his chest. He was uncertain if he slept; he had a sense of the night rushing by. When the sergeant came in and woke them for breakfast, he felt exhausted, as exhausted as if he had spent the night slinging hay bales. The exhaustion forced a measure of resignation, and he trudged to breakfast in a gray state of mind.

After breakfast they were lined in two ranks at attention. A white-haired man strolled into the room, bearing the decorations of two general's stars and a Distinguished Service Cross. A round little belly pressed against his uniform, and under his left arm he carried a steel-tipped swagger stick. For several seconds he stood silently looking over the men before him; then he said, "At ease, gentlemen. I'm Dutch Cota, division commander. I'm sure you all know me." But Heck had never seen him before.

"You have a difficult task ahead," the general said softly, without tension or urgency, like one explaining the rules of a card game. "It is perhaps the most difficult task that the United States Army will ever ask of you. That's saying something, but we should not hesitate to acknowledge the utter seriousness of this matter."

The general pressed the tip of his swagger stick against the wooden floorboards and twisted it slowly. He looked one man in the eye, then another. He looked at Heck, and Heck felt a useless fury. "Let me tell you a little about the man whose actions have brought us here today. His name is Private Eddie D. Slovik, 36896415, Twenty-eighth Division, One hundred and ninth Infantry, Company G. Born February 18, 1920, in Michigan, in Detroit. In 1932 Slovik first came to the attention of the police—he was twelve years old—when he broke into a brass foundry.

From then on he was in trouble, and his police record is a long one: breaking and entering, disturbing the peace, theft, embezzlement, so on and so forth. He was in and out of reform schools, then prison." The general looked at the floor and made a little downward gesture of despair with his free hand. "Maybe it was a mistake for the army to take in a man like this. But, as you know, we are in a war against terrible enemies, and the army cannot now afford to be as selective as it might like. We need everyone to pull their weight, everyone. And, moreover, the army gives everyone a fresh chance. This man's criminal record was forgotten when he became a GI. This man could start new; he could have gone home a hero." The general paused and looked several people in the eye again. "Instead he chose to run away. Not once, but twice, abandoning to their fates good soldiers such as yourselves. He wrote a confession to these desertions. He was offered the chance to return to his position and the matter would have been forgiven, but he refused to return to his rifle company under any circumstances. Refused. He had never even entered combat. He knew the consequences of his actions. A court was convened, considered his case, and now our course is clear."

The general went down the line shaking each man's hand, gazing calmly at them. The floorboards creaked underfoot as he moved from man to man. His grip was surprisingly soft.

That afternoon they were told to take their rifles, and they loaded into the truck again. They drove through town, passing civilians in thick coats who paid them no heed. They turned uphill into the northern slope of the valley. They followed a narrow, frozen streambed, escaped the closely clustered buildings of town, and stopped before a gated stone wall nearly eight feet high. They unloaded and crossed the black, iced stream on an arched footbridge and passed through an elaborate ironwork gate. Before them stood a three-story turreted house, gray with orange shutters, forested slopes rising up behind.

They went inside and were led through spacious rooms of polished wood and crystalline light fixtures. From the walls gazed paintings of stern figures in dark suits. In a small side room they were greeted by a compact, muscular man in a chaplain's uniform. He looked the GIs over and said quietly that the responsibility for this decision lay with a higher authority, and this authority was not theirs to question. Theirs was to carry out orders to the best of their ability. He assured: "The condemned man will arrive here later this evening, and he will have time to prepare himself and his immortal soul before the morning." He said anyone who wished to speak privately with him could, and several of the men did. Heck watched them go in and come out, their grim expressions unchanged.

After a time the lieutenant escorted them through a back door into the garden. To either side were the leafless winter forms of shrubs laid out in symmetrical geometries. The garden was entirely surrounded by a stone wall, and the hillsides rose just beyond. Overhead, the sky was a dull color split by luminous cracks. In an open space before them paths had been shoveled through the snow, like a miniature trench works. The lieutenant lined them up in the position where they would be shooting and described a sequence of events: each soldier's M-1 would be loaded with a single bullet, and one man, selected randomly, would be firing a blank while the others would have live ammunition. This way, theoretically, none of shooters would know if he had fired a killing bullet. From his training, however, Heck knew that a blank didn't cause a gun to kick like live ammunition. Everyone here must have known this, but no one said anything. Some twenty paces away stood a wooden post, about six feet high, where the condemned man would be tied. Behind that a large wooden board had been erected to prevent ricochets. A few feet farther behind was the stone wall, then the mountains.

They went inside again, to a room where they were introduced to a doctor. He was very tall, with a slow, deliberate manner. He told them that they should aim for the heart. He pointed to the smallest man in the firing squad and asked him to step forward and circled with a finger the area where the man's heart was. The doctor asked if there were questions, and one of the soldiers said, "Maybe there should be a piece of paper pinned on there, on Slovik I mean, for a target."

The doctor appeared startled. He did not answer immediately but stood gazing at the place he had circled.

Finally the man he was staring at looked around with a pleading expression. The doctor said, "Seems a little theatrical, doesn't it? Pinning things to a man who's about to die? It seems to me a decent marksman should be able to hit a spot that size pretty easily." He circled the heart once more. "At twenty paces? Isn't that true?"

"Sir," said one man, softly, as if confessing, "at the distance we're shooting from, I suppose I could hit a spinning nickel."

As they drove back to the schoolhouse, a swirling snow had begun to fall.

After supper a few of the men played cards and some of them talked quietly. Heck heard one say, "This duty's rotten."

Another said it was bad enough shooting krauts; he didn't

get into this to shoot his own. "I don't know what I'll do. I might aim high, I don't know."

Heck lay on his bunk listening, and it occurred to him that they—the officers, the army—were afraid no one would shoot. Surely that was the reason the squad was being given these pep talks, rehearsals, these assurances that matters were out of their hands and all that remained was to do their duty. Heck began to hope. He could make a proposal to these men: none of them should shoot when the time came. The army couldn't possibly execute the dozen of them.

But then someone said, "Fuck that." It was the freckled man who had sat beside Heck on the truck. He spit into a can on the floor beside his bunk. "I got no sympathy. No one in my company ever deserted. We're fighting and getting killed. This guy's got no right to walk away from it. I hope I don't get the blank. If ten shots miss high and there's just one in him, I guarantee it'll be mine and it'll be in his heart."

A high, piping wind teased at the windows. A sergeant came with an extra ration of cigarettes for everyone. He said a fearsome blizzard had kicked up outside.

The lights were turned off. Heck lay in the dark and did not sleep nor did he have any desire to. He felt inside himself an awful sickness. He rose and moved through the dark to the bathroom. He stood several minutes over the toilet, expecting to vomit. From the hallway the wind could be heard howling noisily. He came out of the bathroom with his stomach unrelieved. A perfunctory night guard stood duty at the front door, but down the hall and around the corner was a rear door, and no one there. Heck crept back to his bunk, retrieved his rifle and coat, and went out the back door.

A hurtling, frozen wind took the breath from him. He plowed through snow to his knees, around the schoolhouse to the street. The snow-filled night air was a pallid-hued, harsh substance, and he moved over the cobblestones largely by feel, peering uncertainly at the looming shapes of blacked-out buildings to either side.

His plan was vague. But it had occurred to him that he might free Slovik and escape with him. He had no desire to shoot anyone in the course of this, and besides he didn't have any ammunition in his rifle. They would need to commandeer a vehicle. They would go—somewhere. Some isolated farmhouse where French-speaking people would help them. After a couple of days perhaps they would split up, and he could look for Claire—

He turned uphill. He could only barely see the stone wall they had entered earlier that day, and he nearly stepped off the arched bridge into the moatlike stream below. He was grateful to find the iron gate unlocked. At the house an MP opened the door. He looked at Heck and peered into the snowing night. "Who are you?"

"Is the prisoner Slovik here?"

"Did you bring him?"

"Me?"

"Yeah."

"No."

"I thought you might be the one bringing him. We're waiting for him."

"He's not here?"

"He's somewhere between Paris and here, I guess. They're late. The storm's pretty bad. Who are you?"

"The lieutenant sent me."

"Lieutenant Koziak?"

Heck shrugged stiffly. "I'm not certain of the name."

"Well—" said the MP. He blinked blearily at the night.

"Do you think he will be here in time? For things to go as scheduled?"

"No idea. Anything's possible, I guess."

The snow cut innumerable white lines between them. Heck's fingers and feet were numb. He said, "I better go report back to the lieutenant."

"All right. You walked here in this? You want to come in and warm up a minute?"

Heck hesitated, feeling the cold along his limbs.

The MP said, "Come on in."

Heck realized it would be unbearable to stand and try to talk. "I better go."

"Suit yourself."

The door shut and Heck was again enclosed in the snow-filled substance of the night. He was cold and shivering, but told himself these details were irrelevant. His rifle was a weight on his shoulder. He passed through the gate and over the little bridge to the road feeling both relieved Slovik had not been there and disgusted at his relief.

He was on the main street in town, heading toward the schoolhouse, when it occurred to him that he should wait for Slovik to arrive. They might be able to steal the vehicle he arrived in and make off in it.

He stopped on the corner and stood shivering.

But he was too cold, or, as he told himself, too weak. The snow attacked like many tiny vicious animals. He resumed his trudging pace. Besides, Slovik might not arrive at all. The vehicle might have rolled into a ditch. Anything could have happened in this snow.

His thoughts became lost in the bitter rhythm of walking. In his bunk again he cowered under his blankets, rubbed his hands and feet, and soon fell into a deep unconsciousness.

Over breakfast the next morning word was softly passed around that Slovik had arrived. Heck recalled his actions of the night before in a kind of confused horror. In the bathroom he stood over the toilet and disgorged his breakfast. He thought of complaining of illness. But this seemed cowardice. He could see no path before him that was not stained with cowardice.

When they went out to the truck the snow had stopped and the world appeared extraordinarily clean, the air filled with a crisp, blank odor.

They returned to the house with the stone fence and the iron gate. General Cota was there and he gave another little speech, which Heck failed to hear. The men had their M-1s with them, and the lieutenant collected these and took them into another room to be loaded. When he came out he told the men to go in and pick out their rifles by serial number, then await further orders.

They stood holding loaded rifles and wondering who had the blank. The lieutenant had closed the door, and the only window faced a short stretch of snow running to the black-gray of a stone wall. One of the men sniffed and coughed. No one spoke. When the lieutenant returned he appeared to be in a hurry, but once he had lined them up in the hallway he said to wait and vanished again.

The chaplain appeared. He said he had performed a confession and mass for the condemned man. "All that can be done for this man's soul," he said, "has now been done. Also, I have a special personal message from Slovik. He said he doesn't blame you fellows for anything, and you should not feel badly about it. He asked me to tell you he hoped you would shoot straight, to end the matter quickly." The chaplain added, "I don't think any of us wants to see him suffer any longer than necessary."

The chaplain went away; occasional, undefined movements could be heard elsewhere in the house; Heck shuffled his feet and clenched his toes. Time now moved forward no more quickly than the cold moving into his flesh. His breath condensed and bloomed slowly before him. His thoughts dwelled on the color of blood, anticipating it. If the eleven others performed their task, what would it matter whether he did as he was supposed to? It wouldn't matter. Ten bullets were surely enough to kill a man. What difference was there between this task and the task of killing Germans? Shoot the Germans who don't desert, shoot the American who does, sides of a single coin. He thought of the sea-colored eyes of German sniper who had killed Obie and been killed by Conlee and the others.

No, he thought, no. He could not do it. It would be easier to turn the gun on himself. He could not execute a man for doing exactly what he himself had tried to do, except that he hadn't had the courage to be so forthright. He had wanted a wound and an honorable discharge. In Iowa he would have gotten a hero's welcome.

It struck him that he should stride forward, once they were out there, and possibly stop this.

The lieutenant returned and ordered arms at trail. They marched outside and there stood a large group of uniformed officers and MPs, waiting. They stood at ease in a cleared area in the snow behind the firing squad's position. At the post a man stood stiffly, alone, a black hood over his head. It set Heck aback to see the condemned man—he had expected to watch as the deserter was marched out and tied to the post, and he realized now how much he had prized that delay—and the crowd of witnesses further confounded him. This is happening, he told himself, while the steel of his M-1 grew cold under his fingers.

The squad reached the designated position. Weapons were ordered to port and unlocked. Heck couldn't see any reaction in Slovik at the post; if he was nervous he gave no sign. Heck felt himself faced with impossibilities of such scale that it was strange to find himself merely here, in a frozen garden, his fingers cold on the cold gun, the cold creeping inward, the sun pressing down a comfortless winter light. Someone behind him adjusted his feet, creating an extraordinarily loud, crisp scrape and crunch. Over the mountain slopes lay a sun-glowing vapor. Briefly Heck experienced a distanced curiosity, as if he had simply to wait and watch to see what he would himself do, whether he would aim and pull the trigger, a point of question amid a sensation of floating. Behind the squad an officer said, in rapid succession, "Squad, ready. Aim." Despite the speed of the orders—which Heck followed, raising his rifle, guiding the trembling sights of his rifle toward Slovik's imagined heart—there was time enough for the making and dismantling of innumerable decisions. "Fire." And Heck squeezed the trigger in an intimate convulsion. There was a fleeting and terrible omnipotence. And the bullet itself was moving away, the air had an uncommon transparency, and time was drifting down a slant. Soon he was empty of feeling except for a mild curiosity, which perhaps was the elemental emotion, the background color that remains when all the others have been wiped away. With curiosity he watched bullets beat into the flesh of the man tied to the post, watched the body spasm. With curiosity he heard the distorted thunderous noise of twelve rifle shots returning off the hills. He heard, he thought, the echo of his own shot lagging a fraction behind the others. It was a curious thing, that in the time between the shots and the echo of the shots a man could die, that so monumental an event could occur in so trivial a passage.

There was a dull, faded noise of the shots echoing once again off another slope. The deserter hung forward against ropes that bound him to the post. Heck had not had the time, in the combination of the officer's rapid orders and the cold stiffness of trembling hands, to sight carefully, and he knew his shot had been off to the right, perhaps in Slovik's arm. His rifle had kicked and the shell had ejected—the blank had not been in his gun. The echo of the shooting oscillated until finally it surmounted into the firmament, and yet still the echo seemed to resonate in the earth and through Heck's slowly freezing feet. There was nothing else to hear.

The man at the post lurched, tried to straighten, to stand upright, then slumped again into the ropes. Someone behind Heck whispered, "Fuck!" The tall doctor strode out of a little garden shack to the right. No one had shoveled a path between the shack and the post, and the doctor had to high-step through knee-deep snow, with each step crashing though an icy layer beneath the previous night's snowfall. His pace was agonizing. The prisoner once again struggled upright, then fell. The doctor crashed and crashed ahead through the snow. When finally he reached the prisoner, he took a stethoscope from a pocket in his coat.

The officer who had given the order to fire called, "Is he dead?"

"There is a faint heartbeat."

The order was given to reload, and someone—it sounded like the chaplain—said, "Sure, give him another volley if you like it so much."

The major hissed something unintelligible.

The doctor, with the stethoscope in his ears, turned and said, "Please, none of us is enjoying this."

Heck did not understand how anyone could speak a word. But when he was commanded to hold his rifle behind himself, so that he would not see the shell, live fire or blank, that the lieutenant put in, his arms and hands made to obey. The loading of shells was an arduous, infinite process. Someone hissed to the lieutenant that he should not point the weapons at people as he reloaded them. The doctor stood with his stethoscope on the prisoner's chest. Except for the noises the lieutenant made loading the weapons, the quiet was crystalline and nearly visible. Heck was startled by his rifle as it was returned to him. It was heavy and real, and for a moment he believed it would pull him down into the snow.

Then, the rifles reloaded, the lieutenant returned to his position, and a major barked, "Doctor, either pronounce him dead or step back so we can provide another volley, per SOP."

The doctor looked around, slightly startled, or bewildered, as if he thought he'd been alone with the dying man. "No. A second volley won't be necessary," he said. "He's dead."

Breaths steamed out up and down the line of the firing

squad. The lieutenant ordered the squad about and marched them into the house.

They stood waiting in the foyer. Cigarettes were passed around. One man said, "Thank God that's over."

Another said, "He didn't look like no coward out there today, did he? He just stood there and took it."

A GI beside Heck sniffled. The lieutenant came in and told them to go back to the truck. They would get food at the schoolhouse, then be returned to their various units.

They trooped out in ones and twos, without organization. Sitting in the truck, Heck watched the little freckled man who hadn't wanted the blank go vomit into the leafless bushes along the road. Then he got in and sat on the bench beside Heck.

Returned to his squad that night, Heck lay on a wool blanket on the wooden floor of the farmhouse. Conlee nodded to him and said, "Welcome back."

He felt vacant. He didn't feel even a nausea. He tried to move himself toward what had been in the mind of the man under the hood in the moment before he died, the moment when the last heartbeat was heard faintly in the doctor's stethoscope. But he had no access to imagination and could conceive only emptiness.

8.

HECK PASSED FROM THE AGE OF WAR INTO THE AGE OF AFTER the war befogged by unbelief—he knew the war had ended because he was told this, but it was difficult to believe. War was a universe unto itself; it didn't make sense that it could be banished in a moment by the say-so of a few men, the scribble of a few signatures. And he had at some point ceased to think it possible that the war would stop with himself still alive. Only when he read of the bombs dropped over Hiroshima and Nagasaki did he begin to understand that he was not dead, but he was nevertheless in a new world.

Everyone wanted to go home, back to the States, back to Arkansas, Ohio, Pennsylvania, Montana, New Jersey, Georgia, and all the others. Heck didn't understand why, didn't care to think about home or why someone would want to go back. The talk was all of schemes and stratagems for getting released more quickly, and Heck ignored it. He felt he had nowhere to go. To face his father was unimaginable.

At the same time that everyone wanted to leave, the army badly needed people to stay. Large bonuses were offered to anyone willing to remain in the service in Europe. Heck signed up. He was returned to France.

He worked in an office in Amiens, a city north of Paris that had been bombed and attacked by the artillery of both sides. Entire neighborhoods lay in rubble, and people made their homes where they could. The city's Gothic cathedral had survived largely intact, and it brooded huge and dark over the destruction, a blocky shape with a single narrow spire upthrust from it. The stained glass was destroyed, but the statuary had survived; over the front doors were carved hundreds of sinners and saints, the sinners in grotesque contortions as they strained to hold upward the pedestals of the saints. Below the cathedral ran the Somme, carrying a steady flow of garbage.

Heck's work was easy, sorting files, some typing. After typing for an hour or two his wrist would begin to ache where he had been shot. Sometimes he only had to flex it just so, and it would flash with pain. Sometimes minutes would pass unnoticed while he sat gazing at it. He thought of the execution every day, every hour. When he had returned to battle after Slovik's execution, he found he had no fear—or at least he could very easily control himself in spite of it—and fought reasonably well until the end of the war. He didn't understand this change, did not want to understand it, and took no pride in it.

Many in the city had fled and had not yet returned. In places there was no one alive to be seen, and the heaped rubble and the hollow-eyed, roofless buildings on all sides were silent but for the buzzing of flies. A trickle of grim and wary refugees moved through the streets, carrying their things in bags, pushing them in overburdened wheelbarrows and baby carriages. Along some streets the cobblestones had been stolen—pried out one by one and carted away. There were many rats, brazen in their numbers and indifferent to Heck. Around the peripheries of the city wandered packs of stray dogs. Each time Heck saw them, or heard their howls, he wondered what had become of Pooch.

Here and there, however, attempts at clearing the rubble and rebuilding had begun, and people grappled with and reduced the piles, erected new framing, poured concrete, planted trees. Posters for politics and parties of all sorts were plastered onto the walls, and many of the abandoned structures hosted densities of graffiti. The news said that the Russians and Americans were already fighting skirmishes in Berlin. Among the men who Heck worked with, the talk was all of the Russians. The weeks passed in bright, splendid days and gray ones without sun, and these all were much alike to Heck's withdrawn awareness. Certain memories clutched at him again and again, demanding his attention. His hand slipping inside a dead man. Obie stiffening, and the sea-colored eyes of the German who had shot him. The tall soldier exploding. The body of the woman under the bushes. The icicle. It was, however, the memory of Slovik's lurching to life against the post and ropes that struck him most often and most abruptly, like a punishment of his conscience upon him.

Each morning his route to work took him alongside the cathedral and through the plaza before it. Some mornings a forlorn organ grinder swayed in the center of the plaza, grinding a tune slowly. He had a leashed monkey, which danced at his feet with weird abandon. Just past the plaza lay a row of bomb-demolished shops before which the beggars huddled, gathering into themselves as if fearing to take up too much space in the world, their backs hard against broken walls and piles of fallen stones. Many wore ragged suits and coats that had once been finely tailored, or hunched under filthy, ornate shawls. Some of the men still wore their army uniforms. They appeared desiccated, they were missing a foot or a hand or their faces were waxy with burns, they had no eyes or no teeth or no ears. Thin, staring children sat among the women. Tiny infants were bundled in old towels or curtains. Heck offered his coins to the children. Some accepted the coins with grave solemnity; others snatched at the glint of metal like birds, hungry and wary.

One day he noticed a woman among the others watching him with particular intensity. A little swaddled creature sat nestled under her arm, and she did not hold out her hand toward Heck, pleadingly, as the other beggars did. She only gazed at him, undeniably at him, meeting his eyes without any evident expression of anger or hope. He seemed to rise toward knowledge in steps: he thought he knew her; he knew he knew her; he knew her. It was Claire. The child beside her made an odd mewling sound. A man with no legs rocked forward and hissed at him. Empty, upturned hands pushed vaguely toward him. Heck kept walking. She continued to gaze at him. He passed her and felt her gaze still, a soft pressure on his back. He continued walking, walking until he knew she was out of sight. He needed to report to work, and he did.

In the office, a lieutenant snapped his fingers in front of Heck's face to break him from a reverie. He was amazed by himself, by the realization that for months he had ceased to think of

Claire, that he felt no love for her anymore, only a soft pity. As he returned to his quarters that evening he took a longer route to avoid the beggars. The following morning he again took the longer path, and soon the new route, which went under a series of large, disfigured plane trees, had become a habit.

The fervent emotion he had felt toward her during the war was strange to him now. He dug to the bottom of his footlocker searching for the music box, fearing he had lost it. He found it inside a knotted sock. He wound the tiny key and listened to the thin, plinking music and remembered with a feeling of dull sickness his notion, long ago, that if he survived the war he would wander France in restless melancholy, searching for his love.

One day the gardens were full of enormous cabbages. Soon after they were empty of anything but dirt. New poles strung with electric and telephone cables were being erected in the ruined portions of the city. Heck, watching these poles swing up into place, discovered himself trying to understand how a torso might become tangled there. When it rained he watched the rain move wavelike over the streets, and it made him think of the sea and of Claire. Instead of his old passion he felt a somber guilt, and as the days passed this feeling grew stronger. It seemed to him that he had behaved poorly toward Claire, from beginning to end. He wondered also, though, whether it truly had been her he had seen among the beggars. It seemed just as likely to have been delusion.

Nevertheless, he was unsurprised to look over one day and see Albert just across the river, standing at the top of the embankment and watching the gray-brown water. There was only a question of reality. Heck examined the purpled dents in the man's cheeks, his uneven beard, the empty, pinned sleeve. Albert looked up and smirked, very much as if he had expected to see Heck there. "It's you," he called across the water. His eyes were sunken and dark. "Well, won't you come across and join me?"

Heck walked to the next bridge. He thought then of running onward, but the thought embarrassed him, and it had no power. He crossed the bridge and waited for Albert to join him. Soft thin mists hovered over the water of the river, and below these wisps moved occasionally the color of an autumn leaf. Albert was strolling with an odd, forced languor. "I must admit," Albert said as he came up, "I did not expect you would survive. But here you are, just walking along, with two arms, two legs." He stopped and stooped, picked a cigarette butt off the street and put it into his pocket. "You know, you always look very lonely."

He touched Heck's elbow, and they walked on alongside the river. The buildings were of stone and narrow. Fallen foliage lay over the street and smoke rose from the chimneys. It was early morning, and there were few people out. "I saw Claire," Heck said, "among the beggars, some time ago."

"I know. She mentioned it."

"How is she?"

Albert shrugged. "As well as can be expected."

"Ives?"

"Him too."

They walked a time quietly. Heck could hear, faintly, the scuttle of rats pacing them in the shadows below, by the river. Albert said, "Have you any money?"

Heck pulled out the francs he had in his pockets and counted them. In value, it amounted to a little more than a hundred dollars. He held the bundle toward Albert. Albert accepted it and counted with a deft movement of finger and thumb. Then the bundle vanished inside his coat.

Heck asked, "Is there really a child?"

"Her name is Genevieve. Pretty, isn't it?"

"She's not mine, Albert."

"Of course not. She was two months too early to be your child."

Heck thrust his hands into his pockets. He found the music box there, and he gripped it until the corners cut into his fingers. He said, "Whose then?"

"Some damned Nazi." Albert smoothed the scruff of his beard with his hand. He glanced at Heck. "He raped her, of course. But people already thought we were collaborators." He shrugged. "We were struggling for bread each day."

After a moment Heck took the music box from his pocket and held it out. "You'll give this to Claire."

"This," Albert said as he took it. He opened it and closed it with the fingers of his hand. "It was her mother's." He gestured a small, unhappy arc with the music box. Then, abruptly, he shrugged. "Well," he said, and without another word he turned and started back in the direction they had come. Heck, with hands in emptied pockets, watched him go.

He never saw Albert again. He had no idea if what Albert had said was true. Such confusion now appeared to him unsurprising in the fogged world. He often had trouble taking his thoughts to any conclusion. Perhaps he really had seen Albert. Perhaps Claire had had a child by some German. Perhaps they had been collaborators. Perhaps not. Perhaps he might still have loved her, in some other world.

A week after the encounter with Albert the streets were filled with inches of snow. The trucks moving through the city left thick, paired black lines, while men in hats and dark coats on bicycles traced thin, wavering impressions. The snow stood gleaming on the steep roofs. Slovik shuddered and strained in his ropes again, unwilling to accept even the duty to die. Heck returned to the wall of beggars, who were arrayed as on any other day, squatting in the snow and slush in their torn and rag-bound shoes. They looked at Heck without expectation or hope, and Claire wasn't among them. He felt he had deserted her, again. As surely as he had abandoned everything else, he had abandoned her.

Winter took firm hold. The beggars grew fewer, and those who remained were wrapped more deeply into their rags. The radio said that, in Paris, de Gaulle had resigned. The eaves were draped with the shimmer of icicles. People who had homes and offices and shops to go to scurried through the streets, chased by the chill toward warmer doorways, but Heck lingered longer and longer, unmindful of the weather except when the falling snow obscured his view as he examined darkened alleys, shadowed corners, abandoned structures. Sometimes when he had a day free he traveled to towns where he had been during the war, or to other places, selected more or less randomly, and wandered the streets, looking. So, he thought, I am searching for her after all. He saw others who were also searching, people with a flickering gaze, people who were always watching the faces in the street, studying the windows and doorways, looking. It seemed there were a great many of these people, marked by the same probing, yearning gaze.

When he was not working or wandering about, he lay in

bed, smoking. And he was there one day when a knock started him from a listless, inward preoccupation. He thought it might be Albert, hoping for more money. He was glad, and he opened the door eagerly. However, there was no one. He scanned the street, and it was empty and quiet. Dusk had dimmed the sky to a battered yellow. From the far side of the city came the sound of a train tapping slowly along tracks.

Then he heard a soft noise, and he looked down. Beside the doorway was a cardboard box holding a rough bundle of blankets, and among the folds of the blankets was a tiny child, less than a year old. She sat in a kind of collapse, like a sodden towel. Then she peered up at Heck, frowning and blinking. Nestled beside her was the little silver music box. Gently, Heck picked it up and opened it. Inside was a note. "Please, please, Iowa, take her."

In the street a platoon of schoolboys swarmed by, running hard, sliding on patches of ice, hooting and howling to one another. The child in the box, looking up at Heck, drew a rasping breath, raised one arm vaguely, then began to bawl. Heck crouched over the child, but he didn't know what to do. He reached in to try to soothe her, but she began to scream. Her face became a harsh red, ugly, disfigured as if in pain. Her tortured breaths steamed in the cold. She looked very tiny and helpless. Heck looked at the street. He felt the cold in his hands. A light went on in a window at the corner. A door opened. The screams echoed in distortions off the buildings.

AUTHOR'S NOTE

Private Eddie Slovik was executed for the crime of desertion on January 31, 1945. He lay buried in France alongside convicted rapists and murderers in a grave marked only by a number until 1987, when his body was moved to his hometown of Detroit. Eddie Slovik's story was uncovered and told by the journalist and author William Bradford Huie in an excellent book, *The Execution of Private Slovik*.